'Maisie…' Her name was a caress on his tongue.

'I am not the man you think I am, *mia piccola*. You are looking for a white knight and I am not he. I cannot give you what you want.'

'You can.' Oh, he could, he *could*. And who needed a white knight anyway?

'Maisie—' Blaine took a step backwards, away from her '—believe me. This will only end badly.'

She didn't care. She really, *really* didn't care. 'It won't.'

'There are things you don't know,' he replied.

'So tell me.' She faced him, hands on hips. 'Tell me what I don't know.'

Helen Brooks lives in Northamptonshire and is married with three children. As she is a committed Christian, busy housewife and mother, her spare time is at a premium, but her hobbies include reading, swimming, gardening and walking her old, faithful dog. Her long-cherished aspiration to write became a reality when she put pen to paper on reaching the age of forty, and sent the result off to Mills & Boon.

Recent titles by the same author:

THE PASSIONATE HUSBAND
HIS MARRIAGE ULTIMATUM
THE MILLIONAIRE'S PROSPECTIVE WIFE
A RUTHLESS AGREEMENT

THE ITALIAN TYCOON'S BRIDE

BY
HELEN BROOKS

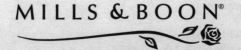

MILLS & BOON®

All the characters in this book have no existence outside the imagination of the author, and have no relation whatsoever to anyone bearing the same name or names. They are not even distantly inspired by any individual known or unknown to the author, and all the incidents are pure invention.

First published in Great Britain 2006
Harlequin Mills & Boon Limited,
Eton House, 18-24 Paradise Road, Richmond, Surrey TW9 1SR

© Helen Brooks 2006

ISBN-13: 978 0 263 84847 2
ISBN-10:   0 263 84847 7

Set in Times Roman 10½ on 12 ¾ pt.
01-0906-54324

Printed and bound in Spain
by Litografia Rosés, S.A., Barcelona

THE ITALIAN
TYCOON'S
BRIDE

CHAPTER ONE

MAISIE sat staring at the navel ring of the spiky-haired girl sitting opposite her on the tube train. It was a very nice piece of jewellery but definitely flamboyant, encrusted as it was with tiny, different coloured stones. Then again its owner was flamboyant; the purple and red striped hair below which sparkled a pair of blue eyes surrounded by panda make-up was meant to catch the attention. *This is me, take it or leave it. No compromise.*

Maisie shifted in her seat, her eyes still locked on the little ring and the tanned flat stomach surrounding it. The girl certainly hadn't pigged out on pizza and toffee doughnuts the night before; in fact Maisie doubted if she had ever pigged out in the whole of her life. The ultra-long legs encased in strategically torn jeans were as thin as any model's, and the cropped vest top showed slim arms heavily weighed down with bangles and beaded bracelets. She looked gorgeously slender and brimming with the joy of life. Technically the girl was very different from the tall willowy blonde whom Jeff had just waltzed off with, but the pair were definitely sisters under the skin.

The thought of Jeff and Camellia—apparently the name meant perfection, one of Maisie's not-so-good friends had taken covert pleasure in informing her—brought tears stinging at the backs of her eyes, and Maisie fumbled for a tissue. She couldn't cry here, not on the tube in the middle of a Saturday morning, she told herself fiercely, turning her head and staring at her reflection in the tube window. This wasn't a good idea. It reminded her that her wavy brown hair and brown eyes were fairly nondescript and that her face was definitely of the round variety.

Possibly because she was concentrating extremely hard on not glancing at the girl across the way again, Maisie realised in the next moment or two that she had missed her stop. Great. Now, on top of acknowledging that everyone probably thought they were sharing the carriage with a fat little munchkin, she was going to be late for her weekly coffee date with Sue and Jackie. And they would be bound to assume it was because she'd been howling over Jeff.

Poor Maisie. They might not say it out loud but that was what they would be thinking. She could read it in everyone's eyes. Well, it was up to her to show them that she wasn't poor Maisie, wasn't it? That she didn't give a damn, in fact? She bet the ringed beauty across the way wouldn't. Not that a girl like her would have her fiancé walk out on her a few weeks before the wedding in the first place.

Determinedly keeping her eyes from straying but employing her brain into the bargain, Maisie alighted at the next stop, eventually emerging into the bright sunlight of a busy Oxford Street. The June sun was hotter than she had expected it to be, and she found herself wishing she had worn something other than her calf-length denim skirt and long-sleeved top as she battled her way through Saturday shoppers.

Why was she breaking her neck to get to a meeting she had no wish to be at?

As the thought struck, Maisie's frantic pace slowed. She

was going to arrive at the coffee bar looking like something the cat wouldn't deign to drag in at this rate, and ten to one Sue and Jackie would be sitting there all cool and relaxed, sipping iced water or something non-calorific.

Not that the pair of them weren't dear friends, Maisie assured herself as she continued at a more measured pace past John Lewis. They had all been inseparable from primary school, but Sue was a successful fashion buyer and Jackie a beautician with her own business, which had come on in leaps and bounds since she'd started it three years ago.

She, on the other hand, had followed her heart and not her head—or, more to the point, her prospective bank balance—in her choice of career. On leaving sixth-form at eighteen with three quite presentable A-levels in chemistry, maths and biology, she'd had to accept that the grades were not the straight As needed for the veterinary degree course she had aspired to. With only six universities in the UK having veterinary schools, and five applicants for every one of the three hundred or so places, she had been presented with the unpleasant truth that she could try for ever and not obtain the necessary qualifications.

Maisie was nearing the coffee bar now and guilt at being late speeded up her feet even as her mind meandered on.

And so, in spite of encouragement from her teachers and even stronger encouragement from her mother to apply for a degree course in biochemistry or animal physiology or even agriculture, she had opted for veterinary nursing. The money was poor, the hours long and, since there was no equivalent to the nursing service within human hospitals, there was no formal career structure and promotion prospects were limited. And she loved every minute. Or she had done until two weeks ago.

'Whew.' She breathed out a sigh as she dived off Oxford

Street into the side street in which the coffee bar was situated, standing by some iron railings as she smoothed her hair back from her hot face, pulled down her top and wished she didn't feel so sticky. After energetically fanning herself with a leaflet for vitamin pills she'd found in her handbag, she conceded it just made her more over-heated. She glanced at her watch. It wasn't the expensive little silver beauty Jeff had given her for Christmas, because that was now the pride and joy of her local charity shop, along with every other gift which had come from him in the two years since she had known him; the ring she had flung back in his lying, cheating face. No, this watch was a sturdy plastic thing from a market stall. Which summed up her entire life at present really.

The rich smell of coffee was overpowering as she stepped through the open doors of the coffee bar, her glance moving swiftly over the assembled clientele. She saw Sue and Jackie in the same moment that both women raised their hands to her, but what made her pause for a second was the fact that they were not alone. A man was sitting lazily beside Jackie, one knee crossed over the other and with both arms stretched out along the back of the booth in which the three were situated. And what a man. Raven-black hair, tanned skin, chiselled features—even from six or seven metres away he was drop dead gorgeous. Not that she was really noticing such things at the present time, of course, not with her life in tatters, she assured herself as she made her way over to them.

'You're twenty minutes late.'

This was from Sue, who was such a stickler for punctuality she had made sure none of them ever got a detention for being late at school.

'Sorry.' Maisie smiled brightly. 'Missed my tube stop.'

'That's fine, no problem.'

As Jackie spoke Maisie saw her flash Sue a glance which said all too clearly, Don't have a go at her; remember what's happened. Poor Maisie.

Maisie kept the smile in place with gritted teeth. 'I'll just go and grab a coffee, won't be a tick.'

'Please, let me. What will you have?'

Drop dead gorgeous had risen to his feet at her approach, and now Jackie said, 'Oh, I'm sorry. I should have introduced you. Maisie, this is my uncle, Blaine Morosini. Blaine, my other best friend, Maisie.'

Uncle? But he was nowhere near old enough to be Jackie's uncle, was he? And then, as Maisie stared into a pair of greeny-blue eyes heavily fringed by black lashes, she found her thoughts moving in a different direction. She didn't consider herself particularly small at five-foot-six, but she was having to look up a considerable way. Blaine Morosini must be at least six-foot-three or -four, and big with it. Well, not big exactly, she amended, answering his formal, 'How do you do?' with a smile and a nod. There didn't seem to be the tiniest bit of fat on the lean broad frame from what she could see. But certainly he was more muscled and honed than most men. Or perhaps it was just that he gave an overall impression which was a bit overwhelming.

She blinked, finding it surprisingly hard to break the hold the beautiful eyes had on her.

'I know what you're thinking, Maisie.'

Jackie was smiling as Maisie's gaze swung to her friend's face. Maisie almost blurted out, If you do, don't say it out loud, before she stopped herself.

'You're thinking, how can Blaine possibly be my uncle when he's only a couple of years older than us, aren't you?'

Maisie breathed a silent sigh of relief. 'Something like that.'

'I'm Jackie's half-uncle, to be strictly accurate.'

Again she was forced to look at him and now the overall width of strong male shoulders registered deep in her body with a definite jolt. That and the smoky rich voice with its curl of an Italian accent.

'And the relationship is quite simple. My brother, Jackie's father, was conceived by our father's first marriage. My father married again many years later and I am the result of this union.'

'I see.' She nodded in what she hoped was a brisk, it's-none-of-my-business fashion. She knew Jackie's father had come over from Italy as a young man because he had quarrelled bitterly with his father. Jackie and her siblings had never met the Italian side of their family; in fact her friend had told her their mother had warned them never to ask questions or speak of their father's homeland. Obviously something had happened recently to change this.

Jackie probably guessed what she was thinking again because now she said quietly, 'My grandfather is very ill but I'll explain later. Come and sit down while Blaine gets you a coffee. What would you like? Your usual?'

Her usual was a large latte, often accompanied by the out-of-this-world coffee cheesecake the coffee bar was famous for. Maisie swallowed. After the pizza and toffee doughnuts she had lain in bed feeling like a beached whale, and had gone to sleep promising herself tomorrow would be the start of a stringent diet. No more comforting herself with the fact she had always been rounded and that some men preferred curvy women; that was what Jeff had said and he had disappeared into the blue with a beanpole. 'A black coffee, please.'

'A black coffee?' Sue, never the most tactful of creatures, fairly screeched in amazement. 'You hate black coffee.'

'I've developed a taste for it recently.' A few hours ago, as it happened. And then, before Sue could say anything else, Maisie added firmly, 'And nothing to eat, thank you. I've just had breakfast. I got up late.'

'Black coffee it is then.'

Blaine's voice was matter-of-fact, but Maisie had the nasty notion that he knew her mouth was watering for the cheesecake. And that told her Jackie had informed him of her recent broken engagement and he had put two and two together and made four. But of course she could be being paranoid here. It was something which was happening fairly frequently recently.

She sat down as Blaine walked away and immediately Sue whispered, 'What do you think of Jackie's uncle, then? A real Italian dreamboat, or what?'

Maisie smiled. She hadn't been looking forward to seeing Sue and Jackie; she hadn't been looking forward to anything, and it felt like she never would again, but now she was glad she had made the effort to come. Sitting here like this, she almost felt normal again instead of the fattest, ugliest, most unfanciable female in the whole of London. 'He's very good-looking,' she agreed quietly.

'Very good-looking? That's like saying the Taj Mahal is a little bit famous. If anyone's got the X-factor, he has. I couldn't believe it when I walked in here and saw him sitting with Jackie. For a minute I thought it was a new boyfriend and I was going to scratch her eyes out. Why you didn't tell me he was coming so I could have made more of an effort, I don't know,' she added in an aside to Jackie. 'I'd have worn something new.'

'Sue, you always look immaculate, besides which this isn't about you,' Jackie said shortly. 'You know the history and all the trouble in the family and the whole thing's very awkward. Blaine arrived from Italy yesterday and, although he's staying with us and Dad's flying out with him tomorrow to see my grandad, they're not getting on that well. I've got the impression Blaine blames my dad for everything that happened although he hasn't said so, not in so many words. Anyway, I persuaded him to come with me today to give Dad breathing space at home, that's all.'

'Blaine isn't Italian, is it?' Maisie asked hastily into the very tense pause which followed. Sue didn't appreciate criticism. 'The name, I mean.'

'His mother's American.' Jackie's dark eyes went to the tall figure now paying for the coffee. 'Which is pretty ironic because, from what I can make out from Mum on the quiet, the main cause of the quarrel between my dad and my grandfather was her. Dad met her when she was on holiday in Italy and they started writing to each other, and then he came to England to see her a couple of times. When my grandfather realised things were serious he hit the roof apparently. Said my dad had to marry a nice Italian girl or he would be disowned, something like that. My dad said fine, disown me, and came over here and married my mum. And that was that.'

Three pairs of eyes watched the pretty redhead at the till, who was fluttering her mascaraed eyelashes at Blaine. As she dimpled up at him he bent closer to hear what she was saying. Maisie's lips curled. Typical man. He was soaking up the attention; they all did. Jeff had. Although, with him, she had been foolish enough to think he was different. Big mistake, but she wouldn't be making it again.

When Blaine turned and glanced their way in the next moment Maisie didn't have time to straighten her face. She saw his eyes narrow as they took in her expression and for an instant she froze, then she turned her head and asked Sue how things were going at work. It was a fail-safe ploy because if there was one thing that Sue loved besides men and chocolate it was her job. She made sure the two of them were deep in conversation when Blaine reached the table, accepting the coffee with a smile and a 'Thank you', before pretending an interest in the latest in-colour and current top designers.

'You are welcome.' It was cool and faintly derisive.

Maisie's stomach did a fairly good imitation of a pancake on Shrove Tuesday and flipped right over. He had seen. But of course he'd seen; she knew that, didn't she? But somehow she had expected him to at least pretend he hadn't noticed she had been looking at him as though he was something just emerging from the slime.

Sue seemed to have lost interest in ribbon belts and bow bags and other accessories one just *had* to have for that perfect outfit this season now Blaine was back. Maisie watched as her friend went into *femme fatale* mode. The last time she had seen this was two years ago at a summer barbecue just after she and Jeff had started dating, and the man Sue had been after then had succumbed even before the kebabs had cooked. Not so with Blaine Morosini. He remained charming and lazily amused but infinitely cool as Sue put the girl at the till to shame in the seduction stakes.

Eventually it seemed Jackie couldn't stand it any more. 'We'd better be going; Mum's expecting us back for lunch,' she said, standing up so abruptly that everyone stared at her for a second.

'OK.' Maisie stood up too, followed by Blaine and then—grudgingly—Sue.

'Heavens, is that the time?' Sue suddenly reverted from Mata Hari mode to career woman. 'I was supposed to be on the other side of Regent's Park by now. We think we've found a wonderful new designer, but if he's as good as one of my staff thinks he is, the other houses will be after him when word gets out. I've managed to persuade him we're doing him a favour by my going along to see his work today. Must fly. Blaine—' she smiled sweetly '—it was *such* a pleasure to meet you. Bye everyone.'

The next moment she was gone in a whirl of flirty chiffon skirt, spaghetti-strap top and expensive perfume.

Blaine spoke into the brief pause. 'And you?' he said softly to Maisie. 'Have you got to rush off to some business appointment or other?'

Perhaps Jackie *hadn't* told him about her situation then, or not the full story at least. She didn't think he was being nasty and that was what it would have been to point out that she didn't have a job as from last night. Jeff hadn't just been her fiancé; he'd been her boss as well and owner of the veterinary practice she had worked at for the last three years. On the same evening she had flung his ring at him and he had told her he was taking a couple of weeks off to 'let everything cool down', she had written her resignation letter and had given it to his secretary the next morning. It had been added confirmation that she had done the right thing when word had filtered through that the two weeks cooling off period for him had involved a holiday somewhere hot with the beanpole.

She had worked her two weeks' notice with an aching heart and a doggedly cheery manner—at work at least—and had left the practice last night without looking back.

She had two interviews lined up for the next week. Veterinary nurses were in increasingly short supply these days— most girls wanted better pay and working conditions than the job offered—and so she wasn't too worried about finding new employment. Just whether she would earn enough to meet the rent. Jeff might have been the biggest rat on two legs but he had been that rare thing in the veterinary world—a vet who paid the least of his staff extremely well. Even his kennel maid earned more than the average experienced veterinary nurse.

Aware that Blaine was waiting for an answer, Maisie forced a bright note into her voice as she said, 'Nothing so exhausting, I'm glad to say.' Refusing to elaborate further, she turned from the greeny-blue gaze to Jackie. 'Give your parents my love, won't you.'

'Why don't you come and have some lunch and give it yourself?' Jackie invited at once. 'Mum was only saying the other day she hasn't seen you for ages.'

Another 'poor Maisie' conversation, no doubt. When she had sent out all the cards informing everyone that the wedding and reception scheduled for the end of August was cancelled, she had known a great deal of sympathy and pity would inevitably follow. She just hadn't realised it would be so hard to cope with. And she *did* appreciate everyone's kindness and concern, she really did, but it was so embarrassing and depressing somehow and increased the feeling of humiliation a hundredfold, besides making her feel she was being smothered.

'Oh, I couldn't,' Maisie said firmly.

'Yes, you could,' said Jackie, equally firmly. 'We're only having a barbecue. It'll be quite relaxed, everyone sitting about in the garden listening to music and enjoying the sun. Light conversation, people dozing off in deckchairs with a glass of wine, nothing heavy.'

Maisie got the distinct impression that Jackie wasn't just trying to reassure her that her broken engagement wouldn't be under discussion, but that there was a definite hint to Blaine to lay off his brother here. It did nothing to reassure her that she wouldn't be better off taking a book to the park and idling the afternoon away under a leafy tree, or even giving the somewhat grotty little bedsit she had rented for the last three years a spring-clean.

As she sought in her mind for a suitably convincing lie to let her off the hook, Jackie took her arm and pulled her out of the coffee bar, leaving Blaine to follow in their wake. 'Please, Maisie,' Jackie whispered, 'come back and stay the afternoon. The atmosphere at home is so bad you could cut it with a knife and it'll be better if everyone has to make an effort to be civil because you're there.'

As an invitation it left a lot to be desired but what could she say? Jackie wasn't the sort of friend who often asked a favour, besides which, in a similar situation she knew Jackie would do the same for her. 'OK,' she said flatly as they walked out of the door into what was fast resembling an oven, 'but I've things to do this evening, all right?' Like wondering if Jeff was back in the country yet and what he would think when he knew she had left, whether he'd care, things like that.

'All right.' Jackie turned round to face Blaine. 'Maisie's coming back,' she said happily.

If Blaine knew the reason for her enthusiasm he didn't show it, his manner easy and his voice lazy as he said, 'That is good. We did not get a chance to converse much, did we, Maisie?' He smiled at her.

Maisie stared at him. She wasn't sure if the glint in his eye was because he was amused at the way Sue had tried to charm him, or that he knew that with or without Sue she wouldn't have put herself out to hold his attention. He was too good-looking, too smooth, too utterly sure of himself; in fact everything she disliked in a man, she told herself vehemently. Anyway she was off men. For good. No more worrying about what she looked like or trying to remain civil when they turned up half an hour late for a date, no more feigning an interest in football. All that could go out of the window now.

So why was she dieting?

That was for her, she told herself. For her own self-satisfaction and sense of worth. Absolutely nothing to do with the male sex at all. No way.

When they walked into Oxford Street and Blaine raised his hand and a taxi skidded to an immediate halt, Maisie wasn't surprised. He was that sort of man.

Blaine helped both women into the taxi and then sat down beside Maisie, who was horrified to discover she was positioned beside him. Ridiculous, truly ridiculous, but she hadn't wanted to be so near him. She tried not to mind that she could feel his thigh against hers and that his arm along the back of the seat seemed curiously intimate.

He was wearing a pale blue shirt with the cuffs folded back and light cotton trousers, and as Maisie breathed in she caught the faint tang of a delicious aftershave. It made her wonder if she'd put on perfume that morning; she couldn't remember. Anyway, now was hardly the time to sniff her wrists to find out.

Her stomach lurched as he stretched out his legs slightly before turning in his seat and addressing Jackie over her head. 'I would like to buy your mother some flowers to thank her for her hospitality. Perhaps you could tell the driver to stop for a moment at an appropriate florist?'

'Yes, of course. There's a nice shop on the outskirts of Bethnal Green; we'll be there shortly and it's only a couple of minutes from home.'

Although Jackie had spoken normally, Maisie could tell that her friend was a little flustered. It made her wonder just how awkward things had been between Jackie's father and his younger brother. Whatever, it looked to be a great afternoon!

'So, Maisie, you have a sensible job which means you do not have to work on a Saturday?' Blaine asked in the next moment in an obvious attempt to make small talk and not because he was really interested in the reply.

Maisie made the mistake of glancing at him as she opened her mouth to reply. Across the table in the booth he had been pretty devastating, an inch or two away the effect was magnified a hundredfold. Her confusion prevented the careful reply she would have given if she hadn't been so flustered—something like, As a veterinary nurse I work every fourth weekend but that's all right, I enjoy it. As it was, she blurted out, 'I don't have a job.'

'No?' Black eyebrows rose. 'You are a lady of leisure?'

He made it sound like a lady of the night. She decided she had been absolutely right in her first impression of Blaine Morosini; the man was a pig. 'I left my last job yesterday,' she said, very stiffly. 'I'm going for a couple of interviews this week, as it happens.'

'I see.'

It was obvious that he didn't but Maisie was blowed if she was going to elaborate. Let him think what he liked.

Jackie, however, had different ideas. 'Maisie is a veterinary nurse,' she said helpfully. 'She's absolutely wonderful with animals, aren't you, Maisie, but owing to a bit of, well, domestic difficulty, she couldn't stay at her job any more.'

This was getting ridiculous. 'My ex-fiancé was also the owner of the practice where I worked,' Maisie said shortly. 'And I can get another job easily enough.'

Blaine nodded. 'I see,' he said again.

And he probably did this time. Unfortunately. Maisie suddenly found Blaine Morosini was the last person in the world she wanted sympathy or pity from. Not that she was going to get any, she found out in the next moment.

'What happens if you do not get another job as easily as you think?' he asked interestedly. 'Would this be a problem?'

Oh, no, of course it wouldn't. I mean, I look like the daughter of a Rothschild, don't I? Dripping diamonds, hair and clothes designer level. Struggling to keep the irritation out of her voice, Maisie said, 'I *will* get a job.'

He studied her with unfathomable eyes. 'This is good,' he said lazily. 'The confidence. I like this.'

She really didn't care what he liked.

It was at this point that Jackie said hastily, 'Here's that shop I spoke of coming up, Blaine.' She leant forward and tapped on the glass separating them from the driver, saying, 'Could you stop here for a minute, please? Outside Bloomingdales, the flower shop on the corner.'

After Blaine had exited the cab the two women sat in silence for some moments before Jackie said in a small voice, 'Sorry.'

Maisie didn't try to pretend she didn't understand. She shrugged, forcing a smile. 'I presume you'd already told him I'd just split from Jeff?'

Jackie nodded. 'No details, though,' she said hastily.

'I'd gathered that.'

'Sorry,' said Jackie again.

'Don't worry.' This time Maisie's smile was natural. Jackie had sounded like a chastised child. 'Jeff *did* dump me, he *is* with Camellia and I *have* left my job without securing another one first. Not the most sensible thing, I know, as your uncle so kindly intimated.'

'You don't like him.'

Did a worm like a blackbird? 'I don't know him,' Maisie prevaricated. Neither did she want to.

'I didn't at first,' Jackie whispered, although apart from the driver, who was reading a newspaper, they were alone. 'Especially because he and Dad haven't hit it off, but the more I've got to know him the more I've found he's just very straightforward. Calls a spade a spade.'

In her fragile state she could do without garden implements and any normal person would realise that. Maisie ignored the fact that she had been moaning to herself all week about being treated with kid gloves by everyone. 'I'll take your word for that,' she said drily.

The flower shop door opened and they watched an enormous bouquet beneath which stretched a pair of legs walk to the taxi. Once inside the vehicle the gigantic bunch of pale lemon roses, white and lemon freesias and Baby's Breath filled all the available space.

'Wow.' Jackie was impressed. 'Mum'll go ape when you give her that.'

Blaine smiled. 'Your mother has been very kind to me.'

Yeah, right. And the fact that a massive bunch of flowers like this might annoy Jackie's dad had nothing to do with it? Immediately the thought materialised, Maisie felt ashamed. She was turning into a right sour crab, she admitted silently. The flowers were a lovely gesture and probably Blaine's motives had been entirely honourable. Probably.

She hadn't been aware she was frowning until Blaine said mildly, 'You do not like flowers, Maisie?'

The delicious Italian accent—and OK, Maisie grudgingly acknowledged, it was sexy too—gave her name a peculiar little twist and she didn't like what it did to her nerve-endings. 'Yes, of course I like flowers,' she said evenly.

'You think these are not right for Jackie's mother?'

'I didn't say that. No, they're fine. I'm sure she will love them.'

'Good.' He settled further in his seat. 'Most women adore being given flowers, I've found.'

And you'd certainly know. She glanced at him and saw the beautiful eyes were laughing at her. Arrogant, irritating man. Maisie turned her head and stared across Jackie out of the window for the remainder of the short journey.

CHAPTER TWO

ONCE at the large semi-detached house where Jackie's parents lived, Maisie found herself relaxing a little. Jackie's mother had oohed and ahhed over the bouquet and Roberto, Jackie's father, hadn't seemed too put out at the obvious attempt to win his wife over. Or, if he was, he wasn't making an issue of it.

Jackie's numerous siblings, all of whom were married and a couple of whom had children of their own, were dotted about the garden in chairs and sun-loungers and the general atmosphere was easy.

'You didn't really need me here,' Maisie murmured to Jackie after Roberto had given both women a glass of wine and ushered them to a swing-seat close to the barbecue, which was glowing nicely. 'There are plenty of people to act as referees between your dad and Blaine.'

Jackie giggled. 'It might come to that. But anyway, I wanted you to have a nice lazy afternoon with people who think you're lovely. Nothing wrong with that, is there?'

'You remembered that Jeff's getting home today,' Maisie said flatly.

It wasn't a question but Jackie nodded anyway. 'The git,' she said, just as flatly.

They watched a couple of sausages turn to cinders and

Roberto's attempt to moderate his language in front of the children as a steak went the same way. 'I don't think I've ever been to a barbecue at your mum and dad's when your dad hasn't cremated the food,' Maisie said after a moment or two when Jackie's mother bustled up and extracted the shrunken black morsels with a pair of tongs. She did it deftly but she'd had lots of practise.

'I know.' Jackie grinned, finishing the last of the wine in her glass and smacking her lips. 'I just hope Blaine doesn't offer to help. I bet he controls a barbecue beautifully. Fancy another glass?' she added, rising to her feet.

'Lovely.' Maisie proffered her own half-full glass. 'Just top it up, would you.'

She watched Jackie walk across to the long table at the side of the patio where all the drink was gradually beginning to sizzle, but when her friend got waylaid by one of her sisters Maisie leant back against the upholstered back of the swing-seat and shut her eyes. This was very pleasant, she admitted to herself, letting the seat move gently to and fro beneath its canopy of bright red linen. There was a small breeze in the garden and, shaded as she was from the blazing heat of the June sun, she felt comfortably warm rather than sticky. And it had been so sweet of Jackie to think of her, to be concerned.

The gorgeously fruity rich red wine she'd consumed thus far had already left her feeling mellow, a result of skipping breakfast in an effort to fast forward the diet, she thought ruefully. She would have to be careful to eat something before she drank any more; Roberto's wine was always delicious but extremely potent and she didn't want to get tipsy. She didn't trust herself at the moment, that she wouldn't get maudlin and burst into tears, and she'd rather die than do that in front of anyone.

As Jackie sat down beside her, Maisie didn't open her eyes as she said, 'Thanks for this, Jackie.'

'I am not Jackie.'

Maisie opened her eyes and sat up so abruptly she was in danger of knocking the glass of wine Blaine was holding out to her all over him. As it was, only a drop fell on to the pale blue shirt. 'Oh, I'm sorry.' Maisie stared at the stain as though it covered a vast expanse.

'It is nothing.' He smiled at her as he handed her the wine. 'Jackie is tied up for the moment so I thought I would keep you company.'

Maisie stared at him. He had her wine, so had Jackie asked him to come and talk to her? Probably. If only to keep Blaine out of her father's hair. Not that Roberto had much hair. Unlike his brother who had plenty, on his body as well as his head. She tore her eyes away from the drift of black at the top of his shirt where a couple of buttons were undone and tried to ignore how his trousers had pulled tight over muscled thighs. She had to make conversation—fast. She couldn't let him suspect even for a moment that she was bothered by him. 'When—' her voice had emerged as a squeak and she took a swallow of wine before she tried again '—when are you flying home?' she said, as though she didn't already know.

'Tomorrow evening.'

She nodded. 'I suppose you're in a hurry to get back and see your father?' she said, before she realised it probably wasn't the most tactful thing in the world to say.

If Blaine objected to being reminded of how ill his father was he gave no sign of it, however, merely inclining his head and saying quietly, 'It was at my mother's wish I came to England to see my brother, but I did not like leaving her at such a difficult time. She has some distance to travel to the hospital each day, and I worry her mind may not always be on her driving.'

Maisie nodded again. Even arrogant irritating pigs were allowed to worry about their mothers, she supposed. 'Couldn't your mother get a cab or maybe have friends drive her?'

'Yes on both counts.' He took a deep swallow from his own glass before he added, his voice wry, 'But my mother has a mind of her own. She does not always listen to reason.'

Neither did his father, if what Jackie had said was true. Blaine certainly had an interesting mix of genes in that very male body of his. 'Jackie said your mother's American.'

'Very American.' It was rueful. 'And my father is very Italian. It made for a stimulating childhood if nothing else. They fight like cat and dog but think the world of each other, nonetheless. I understand Roberto's mother was very different. She was his childhood sweetheart and theirs was a peaceful, tranquil existence. He loved her very much, I know this.'

Did he mind that his father had loved his half-brother's mother so much? He didn't appear to. Maisie took refuge in being a third party. 'And your mother doesn't mind that?'

'Of course not. Luisa had died before they met, long before they met, when Roberto was in his last year of school, in fact.'

That might be the case, but she didn't think she'd like to know that a previous relationship had been so altogether perfect. Not that there were going to be any more relationships or men for her. Not serious ones anyway. Maybe the odd date when she felt better, a no-strings attached type thing, but nothing more than that. Twice now she had been in love and both times had ended in disaster; she'd had enough. Men were a different species, let alone a different sex, and they weren't to be trusted. Any of them.

'You frown an awful lot for such a young woman.'

Maisie found the greeny-blue gaze was fixed hard on her face and she flushed. She would have given a month's supply of chocolate to tell him to mind his own business. As it was he was Jackie's uncle and this was supposed to be a nice friendly afternoon. She took a deep breath and then said sweetly, 'I don't, actually, not usually. It must be the company.' And then smiled to insinuate she'd been joking when they both knew she hadn't.

Blaine shut his eyes, leaning back in the seat as he said lazily, 'Are you always this prickly? No, don't bother to answer that. It is me, is it not? You do not like me for some reason. I sensed this earlier.'

Maisie did not know what to say and so she said nothing but her face turned a deeper shade of beetroot.

'You are very different to how Jackie described you.'

She stared at the handsome face. A loaded statement if ever there was one. She let a few moments tick by and, when she couldn't stand it any more, she said, 'How?'

'How what?' He opened his eyes.

He knew what she was asking. 'How am I different?'

'How long have you got?'

From across the garden Jackie waved gaily. It probably looked as though she and Blaine were having a nice tête-à-tête, Maisie thought grimly. How wrong could you be? 'OK,' she said flatly. 'Let me put it another way. What exactly did Jackie say about me?'

Blaine took a few sips of wine. 'She said you were gentle, warm, kind and easily put upon. And pretty.'

Jackie had made her sound like a cocker spaniel. She eyed Blaine warily. 'And you don't agree with that?'

'I suppose one out of the five holds up.'

She knew she shouldn't be saying this; it was simply asking for trouble to give him more ammunition but she couldn't resist knowing. 'Which is?'

'The last.' He rose to his feet. 'Sit still and I'll get some food.'

The last? The pretty bit. Maisie stared after the broad male back. Did he realise that right at the moment she would rather hear that than the rest? Not that she appreciated the inference that she was aggressive, cold and hard, of course, far from it, but when all was said and done…

Blaine returned in a short while with two plates holding salad, savoury eggs, baked potatoes in their jackets, corn on the cob and several morsels of charcoal masquerading as steak and chicken. 'This was actually the best there was,' he said, when he saw Maisie glance at the plates.

Loyalty to Roberto prevented her from speaking the truth, namely that she wasn't surprised. 'This is lovely.' She really couldn't tell which was the steak or the chicken. 'I can't bear my meat underdone.'

Blaine moved a little piece of porous black substance with his fork. 'Quite.'

'I suppose you're used to Italian cuisine,' Maisie said a little tartly, trying to ignore that when he frowned the hard angles of his face were even more devastatingly attractive.

Blaine put his plate at his feet and picked up his glass with the air of a man who had made a decision. Maisie suspected he wouldn't pick it up again.

'Is that a criticism?' he asked softly. 'Don't you like Italian food?'

She loved it actually, but she'd rather walk naked through the streets of London than admit it to him. She blanked her face and lied through her teeth. 'I don't remember tasting any apart from the odd pizza, and I don't suppose that counts?'

He didn't exactly groan but his expression said it all. It was unfortunate that Jackie chose that moment to stroll over and, having noticed Blaine's plate on the floor, mutter, 'Dad's not the best in the world at barbecues but he tries. Now something like *carpaccio* or *risi e bisi* and he's in his element, isn't he, Maisie? You always love it when Dad cooks, don't you?'

Maisie knew that Jackie was standing up for her father but she couldn't have chosen a worse moment. She didn't dare look at Blaine. There was a pause and then, as two of Jackie's little nephews grabbed her and pulled her off, Blaine murmured, 'Of course, when Jackie was describing you she left out the accomplished liar bit. But I'm impressed. You fooled me for a moment and that is not easy to do, believe me.'

Maisie suddenly found she didn't like this little game they were playing. She didn't lie—not usually, anyway—and neither was she all the other things he'd got her down for. She turned to look him straight in the face and, as she did so, she noticed the sensual mouth was faintly stern and his eyes weren't smiling any more. He hadn't liked being fooled, that much was apparent. It gave her no sense of satisfaction, however. 'I'm not an accomplished liar,' she said painfully. 'I'm not what you think I am at all, actually. It's just that I'm in the middle of something awful and…' Her voice cracked and died.

To her horror she found she couldn't go on, not without bursting into tears anyway. She looked down at her plate and speared a piece of shrivelled black something or other and began to chew.

'I'm sorry.' His voice was very quiet, the accent adding a smoky softness that brought her eyes up to meet his gaze. It was then that she made the mistake of trying to swallow.

The next few minutes got her safely past the awkward

moment with Blaine but created a hundred more in the pandemonium which followed her choking. The meat had lodged so firmly in her windpipe that it took one of Jackie's sisters, an experienced nurse, doing a Heimlich Manoeuvre to remove it. As Anna was built like a brick outhouse with arms as powerful as any wrestler's, Maisie seriously wondered if her ribs were broken once she could breath again.

She was escorted into the house by a concerned Jackie, who managed to do a very good impression of a mother hen with a wayward chick, and once she was in the privacy of Jackie's parents' yellow and turquoise bathroom—something Jackie had long since stopped apologising for—she stared at her face in the mirror. She looked as though she had gone a few rounds with Mike Tyson. Her hair was plastered to her forehead, her eyes were swollen and bulging and the red blotches covering her face and neck were only matched in intensity by her bloodshot eyes.

She sank down on the loo seat, gingerly feeling her ribs. They hurt. But not as much as her pride. She decided that as her eyes had been streaming for the last few minutes it was a good opportunity to have a surreptitious cry because no one would notice any difference.

She felt a bit better afterwards, but not much. After washing her face, she removed the last of the black streaks from her cheeks which her mascara had left with some eye make-up removing pads from the bathroom cabinet. A scrubbed but distinctly the worse for wear reflection peered back at her from the mirror. A few minutes of splashing cold water on her heated skin took the worst of the colour away, however, and after liberally using the moisturising cream the cabinet yielded she rubbed her wet fringe dry and surveyed the result. Better. Not good, but better.

'Maisie?' Jackie's voice sounded from outside the bath-room. 'You OK in there?'

'I'm fine.' Maisie took a deep breath and opened the door. She had to face the lot downstairs at some point and it might as well be now.

Jackie had her poor Maisie face on, but as she was holding a make-up bag along with a comb and brush Maisie forgave her instantly. 'Thought you might need a few running re-pairs,' said Jackie sympathetically. 'Come in to my old room and titivate.' Jackie had moved out of the family nest some years ago but, owing to the fact she often dived back home for an odd weekend when she was short on cash or needed some TLC, her room was a home from home with everything a girl needed.

Once she had applied some eyeliner and mascara Maisie felt happier, and with just a touch of foundation and some gloss on her lips she decided she looked better than when she had first arrived. She then whisked her hair into a high knot on the top of her head, which was cooler, leaving just a few curling tendrils to soften the look.

Right, she was ready. She just hoped everyone pretended to forget what had happened and that she could slip away some time soon.

The barbecue was still going on when she reappeared with Jackie, who insisted on giving her a fresh glass of wine and a new plateful of food, despite her protests that she didn't want any. Maisie was just gazing down at her plate when a male voice spoke in her ear. 'I've been waiting for you,' said Blaine.

'You have?' She stared at him in surprise. 'Why?'

His lips quirked. 'Why do you think?'

'I've absolutely no idea,' she said with perfect honesty.

'Come and sit down.' The swinging seat was occupied by several small children, who looked in danger of upending it, but Blaine led her to two chairs in a corner of the garden under the shade of an old apple tree. Maisie went with him and sat down because it was easier than objecting. 'I wanted to ask you something,' he said once he was seated beside her, a glass of wine in his hand.

She stared at him warily. Suddenly looking presentable again wasn't enough protection.

'Have you had a holiday this year?' he asked coolly.

'What?' She was taken aback and it showed.

'Have you?'

She pulled herself together. 'No.' She was supposed to have been honeymooning in August but she wasn't about to mention that.

'I wondered how you'd feel about combining a holiday with some work for a few weeks?'

She stared at him as though he was mad. 'I don't understand.'

'It's very simple.'

It might be but she wouldn't trust him as far as she could throw him.

'My father is very ill, as you know, and my mother visits the hospital every day, often staying eight or nine hours at a time. There is an excellent hotel virtually next door to the hospital, but as she has a couple of horses and numerous cats and dogs she won't consider staying away overnight. That's where you would come in.'

'Me?'

'I need someone to babysit the animals, someone who is trained and capable. My mother wouldn't tolerate anything less. If you were taking care of the home or, more to the point, her pets, I know I could persuade her to stay most of the time at the hotel. That way she doesn't have the travelling and she's safe, my father sees more of her, the animals have someone who can exercise them and who understands their needs; everyone is happy. This would be very good, yes?' He grinned a fascinatingly sexy grin. 'What do you think?'

The danger signals which had been activated by that grin prevented her from replying immediately. Finally she managed to say, 'From all you've told me about your mother, she would never agree.'

'Ah, but she would. I have already spoken to her.'

She stared at him disbelievingly. 'How? When?'

'That wonderful invention, the telephone. A few minutes ago, when you were in the house.'

She couldn't quite take this in. 'You mean you suggested a total stranger living in her home and looking after her animals and she agreed without even seeing me?'

'You are not a stranger to me, Maisie, and she trusts my judgement.'

His judgement of her hadn't been exactly flattering. Maisie eyed him suspiciously, wondering if she should speak her mind or find out more about this crazy idea—an idea which, she had to admit, she'd been stirred by the minute he'd voiced it. To get right away from everything for a while, to spend some time in the sun doing what she loved best in all the world—taking care of animals—sounded too good to be true. And when something sounded too good to be true, that was usually because it was. 'How long are you thinking of?' she asked carefully.

'That is hard to say.' He frowned thoughtfully. 'My father is due to have heart surgery in the near future. If this is a success it will mean further time in hospital and a period of convalescence. It might be a matter of weeks or even a few months.'

Maisie knew she couldn't ask what would happen if the operation his father was to undergo wasn't a success. Instead she said, 'Surely he'll convalesce at home?'

Blaine shrugged. 'Possibly, but your presence would still relieve my mother of taking care of the animals, which occupies a considerable amount of her time normally. Of course she could still ride if she wishes or take the dogs out, but this would be when she feels it is possible rather than because she has to. You understand? I must mention that your duties would not involve any housework or things of this nature; my mother has a very able but elderly housekeeper who has been with her since I was born. Unfortunately Liliana has no rapport with the animals in the house and is frankly terrified of the horses.'

So she wouldn't be totally alone in a strange country. Maisie's mind was moving rapidly. And things like shopping and so on would be taken care of. Great, a few weeks minus carting a trolley round the local supermarket was a thumbs up. But how could she pay the rent on her bedsit in advance when she didn't have two pennies to rub together? And did he mean that his mother would pay for her ticket to Italy and things of that nature? If all this had only been discussed hastily a few minutes ago, he probably wouldn't know, anyway.

Blaine disabused her of this notion in the next moment. 'All travelling expenses would be taken care of,' he said smoothly, 'and of course you would receive an initial sum of money to take care of any bills or obligations here while you are away. Perhaps we could say until the beginning of September, for argument's sake? And then, of course, you would be paid weekly or monthly—whichever you prefer—during your stay at my mother's home.'

This was happening much too fast. She felt as though she had been caught up in a whirlwind. 'What…what if your mother doesn't like me when she meets me?' Maisie asked a trifle shakily.

'Of course my mother will like you. You are a family friend, are you not?'

His brother's family, actually, and was she the only one here remembering that up until yesterday the two sections of the family had been estranged for umpteen years? Roberto and his father were still estranged, if it came to it. Her head was telling her she was mad to even consider this crazy idea. Her heart was saying she had done all the right things—had been sensible, steady, practical and down-to-earth—for all of her twenty-eight years on this planet and look where it had got her. Nowhere, that was where. And if it didn't work out in Italy she could hightail it home and put it down to experience. Or hormones. Something, anyway.

Another thought hit her and she really didn't know how to even begin to voice this one. She had gathered that Blaine didn't live with his parents, but how far away from the family home was he situated? The last thing she wanted was to run into him every day. She stared into the beautiful eyes which were watching her closely.

No. She couldn't ask. She would just have to hope his home wasn't *too* close. That was when it dawned on her that she was going to go against everything her prudent nature—not to mention her mother—would advise and accept this ridiculous offer. And quickly, before he changed his mind. Just like the girl in the tube would have done. She wouldn't have let such a crazy opportunity slip through her fingers without giving it a try.

Maisie's chin lifted fractionally. 'If you're sure your mother will be in agreement, then thank you,' she said clearly.

'I would like to look after her animals for as long as she thinks fit.'

'Good.' The greeny-blue eyes had been narrowed as they'd assessed her response but now his expression changed and his voice gentled as he said, 'I am glad.'

Three little words. Just three little words, so why did they have the power to send a sharp thrill of something she couldn't name right down to her toes?

'If you give me your mobile number I'll call you when I have made the arrangements,' he said smoothly.

Ah. Slight problem there. 'I've lost my mobile,' she said shortly. To be precise, it had slipped from under her chin, where she'd been balancing it whilst talking and doing the washing-up, straight into the soapy suds. 'But I'll give you my home number.'

'Fine.' He smiled. 'That is settled, then.'

Maisie nodded even as a little voice in her head wondered what on earth she had let herself in for.

CHAPTER THREE

'YOU'RE going *where*? And to do *what*?'

Susan Burns's voice was shrill, and Maisie winced as she held the receiver further away from her ear. She had been expecting something like this, she told herself, and she didn't have to justify her decision to her mother. She was a grown woman, not a schoolgirl. But everything was always a battle.

From the moment her father had walked out on them when she was eight years old and her mother had had to assume the role of a single parent, she had tried to rule Maisie with a rod of iron. She had been that way with her husband to some extent; perhaps that was why he had decided enough was enough and had taken himself off to America, where he'd obtained a very good job in his specialised branch of microbiology, before being killed in a car accident just eighteen months after he'd left England.

Most of the time Maisie went along with her mother's demands, for an easy life, but there had been a few issues over which she'd dug her heels in. The first had been her decision not to apply for a degree course in one of the areas her mother had deemed suitable. The second had been to take up relatively low paid employment simply because she liked the work, and the third—over which her mother was still smarting—had been her resolution not to move up north when her mother had announced her plans to move to Sheffield three years ago. It had been high time to finally cut the umbilical cord. Maisie had seen it clearly, even though her mother had not and probably never would.

'I'm going to Italy for a while to take care of some animals for a branch of Jackie's family,' Maisie repeated patiently. 'It's a good opportunity to get away and assess where I want to go from here. To take stock of my life.'

Her mother snorted. She'd got it down to an art and it was the most irritating sound in the world. 'You would be far better served to move up here with me and get a decent job. You're too old to go gallivanting. Your Aunt Eva only said the other day that this thing with Jeff was probably a sign for you to be here with us all.

Maisie was glad they weren't connected by camera phone. 'Us all' meant her mother's branch of the family, which consisted of three sisters and their families all living in and round about Sheffield. All her aunts were like her mother, and Maisie would have considered it hell on earth to be up there. She had made a rude face but now she took a deep breath and said evenly, 'I don't see it that way and, like I've said before, all my friends are here, Mum. I like living in London.'

'Is that why you're skedaddling off to Italy?'

'I'm going for a couple of months or so—a short break, that's all—and when I come back I'll find another job. It's no big deal.'

'And what if this Italy thing doesn't work out?'

'Then I'll be back sooner than I expected.' Maisie decided to cut the phone call short; a quarrel was brewing and she wasn't in the mood to continue in saintly mode. 'I'll talk to you again in a day or so but I have to go now. OK? Bye, Mum. Take care.' She put down the receiver before her mother could object.

Having been satisfyingly assertive, Maisie sat staring round her bedsit once she had finished the phone call. It was dreary, although she'd tried to make the best of a bad job with bright cushions and pots and throws to brighten the place. The trouble was that it needed some money thrown at it to make it anything like light and modern, and if anyone did have any money they wouldn't choose to live here in the first place. Why spend time and effort on a rented property if you had some spare cash which meant you could perhaps take on a mortgage?

'I don't want to live here any more.' Maisie spoke the words of truth which had been hovering in her subconscious for some time, now she thought about it. With Jeff's ring on her finger and their marriage in view she had thought her days here were numbered. Now she found she wasn't about to compromise.

It was a revelation. But a good one, she decided, after the distinctly iffy ones concerning Jeff and the beanpole. She hadn't engineered this but she had already discussed the rent of the bedsit with Blaine, and she had a hefty cheque in her bag right now to cover her four months sojourn in foreign climes. She wouldn't complicate things by explaining she had decided to move home, but simply bank the money after giving her landlord notice here in the next day or so. And once she was back in England in the autumn she would reconsider her position. London was expensive, horrifically so, and she could easily up sticks and move elsewhere. Not Sheffield—never that—but there were other places where her family wouldn't take over and she would be allowed to live her own life. She would still continue to keep in contact with her real friends like Jackie, and the rest of them didn't matter in the overall scheme of things.

The intrusive ring of the telephone cut short her musings. It could only be her mother, determined to have the last word.

Excusing the words that came to mind by telling herself she hadn't actually voiced them, Maisie snatched up the phone. 'Yes?' she snapped.

There was a succinct pause. 'Something tells me I've rung at an inopportune moment?' Blaine drawled softly.

You'd think he'd done it on purpose. Well, she wasn't sure he hadn't, Maisie snarled to herself. She counted to ten before she said, 'Blaine, sorry. I've just had some milk boil over. You know how it is.' Of course he didn't. He had the air of a man who had never had to do anything domestic for himself in the whole of his life.

'Cocoa?'

'What?'

'The milk. It's eleven o'clock at night. I thought it might be cocoa you were making. I understand it is a passion of you British at bedtime.'

She ignored the curls in her stomach that his intonation of the word passion had caused and breathed through her nose. He was being nasty. She just knew it. Insinuating that she had nothing better to do at night than drink cocoa.

Because her brain wouldn't compute milk and the uses thereof, she said, 'Is there a problem?' Please don't say you have changed your mind, not now I've called my mother.

'No problem,' he said lazily. 'Just to let you know I've reserved your tickets and you're flying out on Tuesday afternoon. I trust you can tie up any loose strings here by then?'

There wasn't enough to merit a knot. 'Absolutely.'

'Good.' A brief pause ensued. 'I'll meet you at the airport and take you to the house.'

'There's no need for that. I can get a taxi.'

'I'm sure you can, Maisie.' It was dry. 'Nevertheless I shall meet you. You are a guest in my country.'

'I'm an employee.' She didn't want him to think she had any expectations.

'Not my employee,' he said silkily.

She floundered, the image of a long lean body and wickedly handsome face flashing on the screen of her mind. 'You…don't have to.'

'I know.' The deep voice and accent was an unfair combination. 'I want to. You are Jackie's dearest friend, after all.'

He was laughing at her. She couldn't see his face but she was sure he was laughing at her. Stiffly now, she said, 'Thank you.'

'Don't mention it.'

This time the throb of amusement was unmistakable. Maisie glared at the receiver. The telephone in the bedsit was antiquated. She had seen the state-of-the-art whizkid mobile phone he'd used earlier—it added insult to injury. 'Goodbye,' she said tightly.

'Goodnight, Maisie.' His tone was easy and relaxed. It told her more blatantly than any words could have done that she could indulge in her little tantrums and he didn't give a damn. And then she realised she'd got it wrong again when he added, 'His loss, Italy's gain. The guy was a fool, Maisie. Don't waste time thinking about him. He isn't worth it.' And the phone went dead.

When Maisie exited Naples airport on Tuesday afternoon she was tired and more than a little apprehensive. It hadn't been until she was actually on the plane that the enormity of what she had let herself in for had hit her, along with the fact that she would be in effect homeless once she returned to England. But that was all right, she told herself firmly as she shaded her eyes with her hand and glanced round for Blaine, berating herself for not buying a pair of decent sunglasses before she left England. A friend was storing her few bits and pieces and personal belongings in a spare room until she returned home, and Sue had been very enthusiastic about Maisie staying with her until she fixed up a job and somewhere to stay. So she wouldn't exactly be destitute. Far from it, in fact, with Blaine's very healthy cheque having plumped up her bank balance, which hopefully would be added to while she was in Italy.

No, her apprehension wasn't caused by the situation she would face when she returned home but by what she would be facing in the immediate future, she thought, watching a sleek and beautiful black Ferrari nose towards her. It wasn't until Blaine called her name that she realised it was his car, however.

Oh, wow… She tried to stop her mouth from falling open as she watched him jump out of the sleek confines of the elegant car.

'Hi, Maisie. Good journey?'

He was wearing an open-necked black shirt and pale cotton trousers, and with his eyes hidden by screamingly expensive sunglasses he was a perfect moving monochrome of black and white. The epitome of Italian manhood, in fact. Jackie had filled her in on the wealth the family enjoyed in Italy, which was considerable due to the successful chain of hotels and cafés Roberto's father owned and which Blaine now managed, and everything about him reflected this as he reached her side. 'Very good, thank you,' she managed evenly as he took her suitcase and sports bag. 'How is your father?'

'Bearing up.'

Probably because they were in Italy his accent seemed more pronounced than it had in England, and as he opened the car door for her she felt ridiculously shy as she slid into the car with an excessive show of leg. She had never been in such a low-slung powerful car before and it felt almost as though they were on a level with the road as Blaine folded himself into the driving seat.

Gathering her skirt chastely round her, Maisie said nervously, 'Thank you for coming to meet me.'

'My pleasure.' He smiled at her before starting the engine and her stomach twirled.

As he drove out of the airport she sat stiffly beside him, her hands unconsciously clenched into two fists on her lap and her back straight. He seemed even more good-looking and overtly sexy than he had in England, and the close intimacy of the car had every nerve in her body twanging. And they had well over an hour's drive in front of them, she thought despairingly. Not that she fancied him, of course—she wasn't *that* stupid—but it was the whole experience that had wound her up—the car, the man, the bright sunshine, the foreign climes…

He drove the car surely and expertly through the busy traffic, which to Maisie's fevered gaze didn't seem to have any rhyme or reason to it. There was a great deal of blaring of horns and screeching tyres, which was less than reassuring, especially as she felt more vulnerable than she'd ever felt in the whole of her life.

'In a little while you will begin to see the beauty of my country,' Blaine assured her as the car weaved and dived through the mêlée all around them. 'I am probably biased, but to me Sorrento is everything that is good about Italy. For centuries it was our best kept secret, contained to just a few privileged foreign travellers, and then Tennessee Williams made it the playground of the affluent and the famous.' He shrugged. 'Fortunately Sorrento's charm cannot be spoilt by excess or those who do not understand her.'

Maisie could detect the delicious aftershave she had smelt before in England, something sharp and sensual, and her voice came out less controlled than she would have liked when she said, 'Surely the jet set's presence is good for the hotel and restaurant business?'

'Of course.' He shrugged again, a very Latin action. 'One cannot have everything in life; isn't that what they say?'

Whoever 'they' were, they'd nearly got it wrong with Blaine, she thought ruefully. Roberto's younger brother might not have *absolutely* everything, but he was well on the way to it. A privileged upbringing in a stunning part of the world, good looks, wealth—Blaine was the original Italian playboy, in fact. Forget being born with a silver spoon in his mouth; he had a whole cutlery set.

The traffic thankfully became a little more orderly as they left the airport behind and as the car gathered speed Maisie was enchanted with what she saw. Dominated by Mount Vesuvius, Naples was everything she'd heard it to be— bustling, alive, full of breathtaking architecture and rich colours. She made up her mind that before she went home she would explore the city. She could always delay her departure by a week or so and book into a cheap hotel for a few nights. She might never come to this part of the world again and now she was here she wanted to explore most of it.

It was as they wound around the peninsular towards Sorrento that Blaine, without glancing at her, said, 'Could you try and relax a little? You're making me feel as though you expect me to run out of petrol or something.'

Maisie had been looking out of the window at the spectacular view that was unfolding, but now her eyes shot to his face. 'I'm perfectly relaxed, thank you,' she said tightly.

He said nothing, simply turning his head for a moment and

glancing meaningfully at her hands, which were still clenched in her lap.

She breathed in deeply. OK, perhaps not then, but Blaine Morosini was not a man you relaxed with easily. Not that she wanted him to guess that it was his close proximity that was keeping her on tenterhooks. Hastily she said, 'It's all a bit unnerving, that's all. Coming to a foreign country to work for someone you haven't seen and not knowing anyone.'

'You know me.'

Well, yeah. Not a great help, actually. That was the main problem, in fact.

His frown smoothed to a quizzical ruffle. 'I will show you the sights while you are here. You would like to see a little of Italy, yes?'

'You don't have to do that,' she said quickly.

'Maisie, I never do anything I do not wish to do.'

Now that she could believe. She opened her mouth to insist that she was here to work first and foremost but he continued seamlessly, 'Besides, my mother would be horrified at the thought that you do not expect to enjoy yourself while you are here. She is very grateful for your services but would not dream of taking advantage of your good nature.'

She looked at him warily. She wasn't sure Blaine thought she did have a good nature. And this smacked of him feeling sorry for her. She wouldn't be at all the sort of female he was used to escorting. Socialites, models, the beautiful and the talented, all exquisitely dressed, no doubt, and all used to caviar and the rest of it—they would be the kind of woman he would be seen out and about with. He was probably looking at her as a little waif and stray and she didn't like it.

She swallowed. 'I think it might be best to see how things

go,' she said carefully. 'Whether your mother wants me to stay, if the animals settle with me…'

'As you wish.'

He didn't sound as if he cared one way or the other, which bore out her supposition. She slanted a look at him under her eyelashes as he concentrated on the winding road ahead. She didn't think she had ever met such a *male* man, she thought uncomfortably. It wasn't just the broad shoulders and muscled arms or the curling black hair visible at the top of his chest through the open-necked shirt, it was *him*, an aura—oh, she couldn't find the words to describe it. But, whatever it was, it was dangerous and all the more powerful for his casual unconsciousness of it.

She turned her head and stared out of the window. Blaine was the very antithesis of Jeff. He was blond and boyish-faced, the sort of man she usually went for. Gary, her first love, had been the same. And they had both been cheating so-and-so's. They'd both been the helpless kind of male too, but she hadn't minded that. She'd enjoyed looking after them and fussing round them. At least that was what she'd told herself at the time.

As the thought struck her eyes narrowed. Neither of them had wanted to look after *her*, she realised with something of a jolt. They wouldn't have dreamt of meeting her like Blaine had done today; they would just have assumed that good old practical, sensible Maisie would have sorted herself out. And she probably would have, she admitted, but that didn't mean it wasn't nice to have someone take charge once in a while.

Why hadn't she realised this before? She frowned to herself as she searched her feelings. Probably because she had been too busy making sure no one tried to tell her what to do or forced their will on her in the way her mother had attempted to do all her life. Subconsciously she had started a pendulum swinging without realising it had gone too far. Her frown deepened. Hell, she hadn't realised she was so mixed up.

'Are you hungry?'

'What?' She came out of her reverie to the sound of Blaine's voice and blushed scarlet as though he'd been privy to her thoughts. 'Oh, a little. Not too bad.'

'I'm starving.'

They were climbing high above the blue waters of the Bay of Naples now and had just passed a tiny village of ter-racotta-roofed stone houses clinging to the cliffs. Citrus orchards, vineyards and olive groves were becoming apparent in the golden sunshine bathing the southern coastline.

'There's a wonderful old inn on this road where I eat some-times; they serve the best fish and crustaceans in the world. We'll stop there. You like seafood?' he added as an afterthought.

Maisie smiled. No one could accuse Blaine of being a helpless male, that was for sure. 'Yes, I do.'

'Good.'

He smiled at her, just a quick smile before his eyes returned to the windscreen, but Maisie found her heart was pounding and it horrified her. What was the matter with her? she asked herself silently. She was broken-hearted over Jeff, wasn't she? So how could another man's smile—a man she didn't even *like*—make her heart race and her senses heighten in what was a definitely sensual way? Certainly she had never had this problem with Jeff or anyone else for that matter. In fact, she had always considered herself rather a cold fish sexually. It certainly hadn't involved an enormous amount of sacrifice on her part when she had kept any lovemaking to boundaries that did not involve full intercourse. She had always felt that ultimate commitment was for marriage and, although most of her friends had thought she was mad, she'd stuck to her guns on the issue with both Gary and Jeff, neither of whom had seemed to mind too much. She couldn't see Blaine Morosini accepting such stipulations from any of his girlfriends, though. She glanced at him again, her eyes registering the way his trousers pulled tight across lean hips in the confines of the car, accentuating his flagrant masculinity. She suddenly felt hot.

By the time they arrived at the inn, situated on a vertiginous slope, its window-boxes blazing with bougainvillea and bright red geraniums, Maisie was glad to get out of the Ferrari. She didn't know if it was the car or what, but she had never been so conscious of every tiny movement from another human being in the whole of her life and it was not conducive to easy conversation or relaxed travelling.

Sorrento was only a short distance away now, however, and once fortified by a good meal she could keep her thoughts under control until she was safely at Blaine's mother's house. She hoped.

In view of her suddenly improved bank balance she had splashed out and bought a couple of new things before she'd left, the first new clothes she had had in ages. Green had always suited her warm colouring and brown hair, and as they walked up the steps leading to the front door of the inn Maisie was glad she'd decided to wear the pale green gypsy skirt and delicate fitted chiffon top in a mixture of greens and browns to travel in. She probably wouldn't eat out with Blaine ever again and she wanted to look…nice.

Once inside the inn she found the view from the big shuttered windows was tranquil and the glass of wine Blaine placed in her hand was like the nectar of the gods. They had been seated at a little table for two by the smiling inn-keeper and she sensed immediately that Blaine was a favoured customer.

'This is lovely.' She absorbed her surroundings like a child at a wonderful birthday party. 'It's so utterly Italian.'

Blaine nodded gravely. 'I've always thought so,' he said seriously and then, as he caught her eye, he allowed his mouth to twist in a smile. 'You will love Italy,' he assured her softly. 'It's a passionate country, warm and vibrant and emotional.'

She stared at him. 'Do you consider yourself more Italian than American?' she asked curiously, wondering how his mother would feel about that.

The raven head tilted as he considered. 'I think so,' he said thoughtfully. 'I've always lived in Italy, of course, but several times a year I've taken trips to America to see my maternal grandparents and aunts and uncles and so on. It is certainly my second home. But Italy is my lifeblood; it sings through my veins like rich red wine. You know?'

Maisie shook her head. 'Not really. I'm just an ordinary English girl,' she said, half jokingly.

He frowned. 'Do not say that. That you are ordinary.'

She looked at him in surprise. 'But I am.'

'I do not think so.' The greeny-blue eyes were almost luminescent. 'The other friend of Jackie, the girl who was with us in the coffee bar, her name escapes me—'

'Sue.' It felt indescribably good that he'd forgotten Sue's name, which she knew was horribly bitchy.

'Ah, yes, Sue. Now Sue is an ordinary girl. Articulate, attractive, independent, successful—'

He needn't spoil it.

'But without that spark.'

'Spark?' She didn't have the faintest idea what he was talking about.

He raised an eyebrow. 'Are you fishing for compliments?'

'No.' She glared at him over her wineglass. 'Of course not. I don't know what you mean, that's all.'

'Perhaps that's the secret.'

He was talking in riddles and her stomach was rumbling. She'd discovered since she had been in the inn and smelt the food that she was, in fact, ravenously hungry. Her brow wrinkled. 'Secret?'

'No matter.' He looked at her quietly as a waiter appeared at their elbow with two menus. Once he had departed and she gazed helplessly at the writing, which was all in Italian—only to be expected, of course—Blaine said, 'Would you like me to choose something delicious for you? As I said, I eat here fairly often and I'm used to the various dishes.'

'Thank you.' He probably knew she couldn't speak a word of his language, so Maisie said, 'I was never any good at languages at school; it was the sciences that grabbed me.'

'Interesting.' His eyes laughed at her. 'And lucky sciences.'

Was he flirting with her? Maisie stared at him uncertainly. But then Italian men flirted all the time, didn't they? Of course Roberto didn't but he was Jackie's father and therefore relegated into a different strata. She gave a tentative smile.

'I will have to teach you some basic Italian while you are here, yes?'

Umm, probably no.

'Polite words, of course—thank you, please, how to ask for directions if you are lost, that sort of thing. And the casual brush-off to unwanted suitors. That might not be quite so polite.'

He was definitely flirting with her. Maisie refused to acknowledge how captivating it was to have a man like Blaine flirting with her, telling herself that as she was the only woman present it wasn't quite such a triumph. Any port in a storm sort of thing.

The waiter appeared again and Blaine fired off an order in rapid Italian, which still managed to sound utterly soft and enchanting. It really was a gorgeous language. Like the country. And the men. The last thought jolted Maisie into realising she hadn't eaten a thing since breakfast—thanks to the euphoria of losing six pounds in as many days she'd been motivated to starve herself some more—and the glass of wine in her hand was empty. She had also had two gin and tonics on the plane to steady her nerves—perhaps not such a good idea with hindsight.

Another glass of wine appeared in front of her like magic. Obviously Blaine had seen her empty glass when he had ordered the food. Not wishing his mother's first impression of her to be one where she was carried into the house like a sack of coal, Maisie left it exactly where it was, saying, 'What is it we're eating?'

'We are making the most of the fresh fish by having two courses where seafood features. Not exactly the done thing, I know, but…' He gave another of his Latin shrugs and she wondered if he knew quite what it did to her. 'We begin with *carpaccio di tonno*, which is essentially cooked peeled crayfish and very thin slices of fresh raw tuna on a bed of lemon iced salad sprigs. Following this I have chosen *linguine all'aragosta* because the lobster here is second to none. In most restaurants you would be lucky to get a few mouthfuls of lobster with the pasta but here even I am satisfied.'

Maisie nodded as though she knew exactly what he was talking about.

'Ah, the appetisers.' As the waiter reappeared with several small plates holding delectable-looking morsels, Blaine thanked him, adding to Maisie, 'The Italian word for appetiser is *antipasto*, *sì*? This is your first lesson, *mia piccola*.'

He was becoming more Italian by the moment. And more irresistible. Something told her not to ask what the last two words meant. Instead she tucked into the appetisers and discovered they were absolutely delicious. As was the rest of the meal when it came.

Maisie had always liked her food and made no apology for it, although she would have loved to wave a magic wand, of course, and eat what she wanted without it showing on her waistline. Somehow she had never quite managed the knack of surviving on lettuce leaves and brown rice and all the other things which were devoid of cream and butter and everything that made life worth living, though. Halfway through the meal she decided to put the diet on hold until she was back in England. Time enough then for being miserable. She was well overdue a bit of pleasure with all she'd gone through in the last few weeks.

She did refuse dessert though. Not through any misguided and belated feeling of guilt but simply because she couldn't eat another thing after the most wonderful lobster since the beginning of time.

'You eat like a true Italian.'

They were sitting having coffee and Maisie was wondering how she was going to waddle out to the car when Blaine spoke. She looked at him warily. 'Meaning?'

'You enjoy your food. I cannot bear to sit and watch a woman move the food about her plate as though it is going to poison her.'

But he had probably been sufficiently attracted by their slim nubile bodies to take them out in the first place. Maisie acknowledged the waistband of her skirt was threatening to split. She had been thrilled to bits to find she could actually fit into a size twelve for the first time in years when she had gone on her shopping spree, even though it had been a bit of a near thing between that and the size fourteen. She wrinkled her small nose. 'I'm not fashionably thin,' she said, stating the obvious. 'Jeff, my ex, went off with a size eight blonde who's recently had breast enhancements.' And then she wondered why on earth she had told him that.

He folded his arms over his chest, studying her with an air of quiet interest. 'That must have been hard for you.'

In a nutshell, yes. She tried to inject a note of nonchalance into her voice. 'It obviously wasn't meant to be.'

'No, it wasn't.'

Not into comforting words and polite platitudes, then. Although he had only agreed with her, she found herself bristling. 'Actually, we were very well matched.'

He raised cryptic eyebrows.

'We both love animals and long walks and good food,' she said determinedly, 'and going to the theatre and lazy Sundays...' What else? She knew there was more.

'So does most of the population,' said Blaine, his mouth curving.

'We would have been very happy together.'

'I doubt that.'

'Oh, really?' Maisie glared at him. 'Why is that?'

'Because if he was fool enough to let you go in the first place he would not have had sufficient fire to match you flame for flame,' Blaine said with lazy coolness. 'Fire and water never mix and this is the cause of many divorces. Passion must be met by equal passion or one partner will be left feeling unfulfilled and the other believing they haven't measured up. This Jeff sounds like a water person to me.'

'You don't know him,' she snapped while secretly thrilled that he thought she was a fire person. She wasn't at all sure she was but she was glad he thought so.

'I don't have to. If he had fulfilled all he should have done you wouldn't be like you are now at his going. You would be devastated, distraught—'

'I was. I *am*!' She was furious. 'Just because I don't wear my heart on my sleeve, it doesn't mean I'm not upset, does it.'

'He did not touch the core of you, Maisie. Face it. He didn't have what it takes. If you had married him you would both have been miserable in time. Maybe this size eight, breast-enhanced female is what he needs.'

'So he did the right thing in starting an affair behind my back when we were due to be married in a few weeks' time? Is that what you're saying?' She couldn't remember when she had been more mad.

'I didn't say that.'

His cool aplomb made her wish she had some wine in her glass so she could have flung it at him. As it was, she ground out, 'That's exactly what you said.'

'No, I did not.' He leant forward, his eyes holding hers as he said very softly but with deadly intent, 'Listen to me and stop behaving like a child unless you want me to treat you like one and put you over my knee. I said you were well rid of the guy and you are, and perhaps this other woman will suit him. Perhaps she's as shallow as he is; I really don't know. What I do know is that I am glad you found out what he was really like before you went through a marriage and all that entails. I have been there and when things go wrong it can be ugly. I am glad you are not with this man but I am sorry for the hurt you have suffered. OK? But if he had fully had your heart it would have been worse, I stand by that.'

She stared at him, the anger dying. The man in front of her now was not the smooth controlled Blaine she had seen thus far; this man was quite a different individual. The chiselled cheekbones were taut, the sensual mouth grim and the eyes weren't smiling. Whoever it was he had been speaking about, whoever the woman was that he had loved and lost, she had meant a great deal to him. Maisie didn't know what to say. 'I'm sorry.' She kept her gaze on his face and her eyes were dark and steady. 'I didn't mean to revive bad memories for you.'

His eyes held hers for a moment more and then, as she watched, it was as though he pulled a mask over his face. He settled back in his seat. 'You didn't.' He smiled. 'We were talking about you, remember?'

She wasn't so sure about that but she let it pass, finishing her coffee as he strolled over to the inn-keeper and chatted for a moment or two as he paid the bill. He came back to the table, pulling out her chair for her with the courtesy she realised was an integral part of him. He was the sort of man who would open doors for the woman he was with, stand back and let her precede him into a room, throw his cloak down over a puddle so she didn't get her feet wet. The last was going a bit far but Maisie made no apology for it because it fitted somehow. She wasn't so sure about the being treated as a child and put over his knee, but even that might have certain advantages. She blushed to herself and was glad of the cooler evening air as they stepped out of the inn.

He took her elbow as they walked down the steps to the Ferrari, but before he opened the car door he turned her to face him. 'Let go of what won't be.' He touched the edge of her mouth with his finger and she had to steel herself not to tremble. His voice was deep and smoky when, after opening the door and helping her inside, he leant with both hands on the roof and said softly, 'Take life and embrace it, *mia piccola*. There will be other men, other loves. It would be a crime to waste your youth believing this is not so.'

He shut the door then and walked round the bonnet, sliding into the car and starting the engine without looking at her again.

He had spoken as though he was aeons older than her. Maisie sat quietly with her hands folded in her lap but her mind was racing. What on earth had gone on with this woman for it to have affected him so deeply? Who was she? Was she still a part of his life?

As they drove on and reached Sorrento the sun-baked buildings with faded pink and ochre walls ablaze with vivid window-boxes in the maze of streets of the town failed to hold Maisie's attention as they would have earlier. She could see Sorrento was quaint, colourful and romantic and full of southern earthy charm, the panoramic views awe-inspiring and the pretty piazzas and shops fascinating. But not as fascinating as the man sitting beside her.

Blaine pointed out this and that as they drove on towards the Sant'Agnello district of Sorrento, where orange groves perfumed the air and where his parents' villa was situated, but his talk was impersonal now, distant even, as though he was regretting revealing too much. Not that he'd told her anything at all really, Maisie thought regretfully, even as she reminded herself that she wasn't here to wonder about Jackie's young uncle but to do a job for his mother. She was an employee and that was all.

She continued to give herself a silent talking-to as they turned into what was little more than a shady lane a few minutes later, at the end of which she could see a large white building partially obscured by trees. Almost immediately they passed through wide open wrought iron gates set in a stone wall, then the view opened up to reveal a gleaming white two-storey house flanked by rows of cypress trees. It was bigger than she had expected, a wide veranda with a red-tiled roof running the length of the house.

'All the ground is at the back of the house,' Blaine said as he parked the car on the stretch of pebbled drive beyond the stone wall. 'There is a large garden but most of the land is given over to a paddock and stables with orange groves behind them. I was born in this house; it's very beautiful.'

'Yes, it is.' Maisie jumped in quickly before the conversation moved on. 'Where do you live now?' she asked with what she hoped sounded like polite interest.

'I have a place in the hills above Positano; it is not too far away,' he said as he exited the car. Helping her out a moment later, he added, 'You must come and see it one day.'

'I'd like that.' An understatement. She would just *love* to see his home, she admitted to herself, trying to ignore how his height and the lean breadth of him dwarfed her.

He had put his sunglasses on to drive and now she couldn't see his eyes as he said, 'Come to dinner one evening. My home is at its best on a summer's evening.'

Her stomach tumbled. All the way from the inn she had been regretting her earlier rebuff when he had offered to show her the sights during her stay; now she couldn't gauge if his offer was a polite empty one or if he really meant it.

The large ornate door of the house opened in the next moment, revealing a small wizened woman with snowy white hair standing in the gap. Was this his mother? She was nothing like she'd expected, Maisie thought in surprise, only to realise her mistake when Blaine said, 'Liliana, here is Maisie,' as he held out a hand to the little figure.

'Welcome, welcome.' Liliana smiled at her. 'I have a tray

prepared for you, just a cool drink and some fruit. Blaine said you would be eating earlier.'

Maisie was heartily relieved to hear Liliana speak such fluent English. She had assumed the housekeeper would probably have a smattering of the language as Blaine's mother was American, and as her knowledge of Italian was non-existent she'd hoped they'd get by, but this was better than she had expected. She smiled widely at the black-clad little woman. 'Thank you very much, that's very kind of you.'

'Are you staying for a while, Blaine?' Liliana asked, in the way a mother would rather than a housekeeper. Maisie got the feeling the two of them were very close.

'Not tonight, work calls.' He smiled and touched one heavily lined cheek with his lips. 'I shall bring Maisie's bags in and then leave her in your capable hands, *sì*? Any news from the hospital?'

'He is resting and your mother has agreed to stay at the hotel from tomorrow onwards. She wants to meet Maisie tonight and then show her the horses and explain the routine and feeding of the animals tomorrow. As though I couldn't have done that.' Liliana sniffed. 'Jennifer won't be home for some time,' she added to Maisie, 'so I'll show you your room in a moment and you can freshen up before you eat.'

All the time Liliana had been talking the sound of barks and whines had filtered through the house. Now, as Maisie stepped into what was a wide and gracious hall with beautiful marble tiles on the floor and a curved staircase, the sound rose in intensity. Two large Persian cats were sitting at the foot of the stairs and they eyed her with mild curiosity and another cat, a little tabby, came winding round Maisie's legs as she looked about her.

'These are some of your charges.' Blaine had just arrived

back in the house with her case and bags. 'There are six more cats, mostly rescue animals. My mother supports a local sanctuary and every time she visits them she seems to come back with another cat. The dogs are a mixed bunch too, but quite well behaved on the whole.'

Liliana made a sound somewhere between a snort and a sniff at this point. Maisie gathered that she didn't agree. 'Can I see the dogs?' she asked eagerly.

'Now?' Liliana asked in surprise. She clearly couldn't understand the interest. 'Would you not prefer to freshen up first?'

Blaine, however, was walking towards a door at the far end of the hall and as he opened it a number of dogs tumbled out into the hall. Big ones, little ones, long-haired, short-haired, they all made a dash towards her but instead of jumping up as she had expected sat in an orderly circle once they reached her. All except for one little funny-looking mongrel with big ears and a whiskered chin. He seemed as though he was on springs and kept up a frenzied jumping on the edge of the crowd.

Once the initial onslaught had ceased Maisie counted seven dogs, mostly mongrels from what she could see, although there was a little Scottie and a Labrador in the pack. She fussed them all enthusiastically and, apart from a little shoving and jostling amongst themselves, they behaved remarkably well, although the jumping bean positioned himself on her foot once she straightened again.

'That's Humphrey,' said Blaine, his accent making the very English name sound even cuter. 'He's a law unto himself and the bane of Liliana's life. Isn't that right, Liliana?'

Liliana frowned at him. 'This is not something that is amusing,' she said severely. 'He is a bad dog. Only today he has chewed one of my best shoes.'

Blaine grinned. 'He only does it to get your attention; isn't that what mother says? If you would only love him he would be quite content. Surely you can open up your heart and make room for one little dog?'

'Hmph!' Liliana eyed him darkly. 'You do not live with this animal, Blaine, and my heart is quite open enough, thank you. It does not need filling with dogs and cats.'

'Hard woman.' Blaine winked at Maisie as he picked up her things and walked to the stairs. 'Which guest room, Liliana?'

'The blue.' Liliana ushered Maisie after Blaine. 'Come and see your room.'

Maisie felt distinctly odd as she followed Blaine up the winding staircase. The little exchange with the housekeeper had revealed yet another side to him and this one was perhaps more disturbing than the others. He had seemed almost tender with the small woman and his teasing had been gently affectionate. There had been nothing of the egotistical playboy about him then. In fact, she had found herself envying Liliana, which was perfectly ridiculous!

The blue room turned out to be more of a small suite overlooking the grounds at the back of the house. It held a small sitting room with a two-seater sofa, bookcase, TV and coffee table, and beyond this a large double bedroom with its own *en suite* bathroom in cream and blue marble. Maisie was quite overwhelmed. 'But I didn't expect anything like this,' she stammered. 'I'm here to work; I'm not a guest. This is just lovely.'

Liliana had been looking hard at her and now she suddenly smiled. It was an amazing smile which lit up her face. Maisie realised the small woman must have been beautiful in her youth. 'This is a good girl,' she pronounced to Blaine, who was standing with his back to the window staring at the pair of them with unfathomable eyes. 'I like your Maisie.'

'The lady in question would object to being called my

anything,' Blaine drawled lazily, moving across the room as he spoke and touching the housekeeper's arm as he passed her. 'I will leave you two to get to know each other. Goodnight, Liliana. Maisie.'

'Oh. Good…goodnight.' The suddenness of his departure had taken Maisie aback.

Liliana followed Blaine out of the room. 'I will leave you to unpack and freshen up,' she said quietly. 'Come downstairs when you are ready and we can have a glass of lemonade on the veranda. I am glad you are here, *signorina*.'

'Thank you.'

Maisie stood for a moment, looking at the door Liliana had closed behind her. Was there more to those last words than just face value? she thought. The tone of Liliana's voice could lead her to believe so. And then she shook her head at herself. Liliana spoke wonderful English but she was Italian through and through; it was just the older woman's inflexion which had thrown her. It had been a polite welcome, that was all. How could it possibly be anything more?

CHAPTER FOUR

BY THE time Blaine's mother arrived home much later that evening Liliana had shown Maisie all over the beautiful house and well-kept grounds. Of her own volition she had met the two horses, a stallion and a mare, both with coats as black as jet and liquid, heavily lashed eyes. She had been surprised to see the mare was heavily pregnant; no one had mentioned this thus far. After giving them a couple of sugar lumps to make friends, she had stood watching them for some time, Liliana long since having returned to her kitchen.

The evening shadows turned from gentle violet and mauve to velvet charcoal as she stood observing the two horses, the stallion standing with the mare half leaning against him, their two heads nuzzling every so often.

The air carried the delicate perfume of the orange groves beyond the horses' paddock and stables and it was very quiet and tranquil, the sky pierced with stars and the heat of the day mellowed to a warm breeze.

Something in the stallion's attitude to the mare touched Maisie deeply. He was protective of her, as though he sensed her time was nearly upon her and that she was carrying his foal. He probably did. Maisie was of the opinion that all animals, but especially horses and dogs, knew far more than human beings gave them credit for. They were also a lot nicer than some people she could name.

The thought of Jeff spoilt the peacefulness and, cross with herself for allowing him to intrude at such a moment, she turned and began walking back to the house. She had almost reached it when a tall woman dressed casually in a shirt and jeans came out on the veranda from the sitting room French windows.

'You must be Maisie.' The woman stretched out her hand, her attractive face breaking into a warm smile. 'I'm Jenny, Blaine's mother. I'm sorry I wasn't here to greet you personally but you know how things are. I can't thank you enough for agreeing to come and look after the children for the next little while.' The American accent was a strong southern drawl.

For a startled moment Maisie wondered if there was something Blaine hadn't told her, then she realised his mother was referring to her animals. 'I ought to be thanking you,' she said as they shook hands. 'You've already made me so welcome. I don't feel I'm here to do a job.'

'Good.' Blaine's mother's smile widened, her greeny-blue eyes just like her sons. 'That's as it should be. Look, I'm going to have to leave very early in the morning; they've brought Guiseppe's operation forward. Roberto is with him now and I've called Blaine to go and see him tonight. Just…in case.'

Maisie nodded. She was glad she was here but the circumstances which made it necessary were awful.

'I need to tell you all about the animals—exercise, feeding and so on. I'm afraid, because some of them had poor starts in life, they've got little idiosyncrasies and so on. Nothing you won't be able to handle, but it's better you know.'

Jenny rubbed her hand across her forehead and it struck Maisie that Blaine's mother was tired—very tired. She was the sort of woman who just got on with things, though; that much was obvious already. 'I'll handle everything just fine. Blaine told you I'm a veterinary nurse?'

Jenny nodded. 'Just as well, because Liliana won't be of any help,' she said ruefully, indicating a seat on the veranda and, once Maisie had sat down, sitting down herself. 'Oh, don't get me wrong, she's a swell housekeeper and a dear friend, but on the subject of the children we have to differ. Normally it doesn't matter but it's proved to be a bit of a problem in recent weeks. She can just about tolerate the dogs and cats, although she won't feed them unless she absolutely has to, but she's terrified of the horses and nothing I can do will make her go anywhere near them. And they're such sweet babies too.'

Maisie remembered the stallion's height and lethal hooves. Sweet he might be, a baby he wasn't. But on the subject of babies… 'I saw the mare is due to foal soon?'

Jenny nodded. 'I have to admit that with all this with Guiseppe I didn't realise for a time, then it's just got swept aside. I don't think I've even told Blaine. But my vet is excellent. I'm sure nothing will happen yet but if you were worried at any point he would come immediately. His name and number are on the notes I've left for you. Shall I get them and then we can go through everything?' she added, stifling a yawn as she spoke.

'You look exhausted,' Maisie said gently. 'If you'd rather we could do it in the morning when you're fresher.'

'But I'm leaving very early. I shall breakfast about six.'

'I'm an early bird normally, always have been. You can fill me in while we eat if you like.'

'That'd be great.' Jenny looked at her a little helplessly.

'And please, don't worry about anything here. I promise you everything will be under control, OK? I won't let you down. Just concentrate on getting your husband well. It's absolutely right you're with him at a time like this, and soon both of you will be home and this will seem like a bad dream.' Maisie found herself patting Blaine's mother's hand. 'Try and get some sleep now.'

Jenny tried to smile but her tired eyes filled with tears. 'I don't think I've slept for weeks,' she admitted shakily.

'Come on.' As Maisie helped Jenny to her feet she found herself thinking that she would never have believed she'd be in this position a week ago—a strange country, a strange house and she was providing the shoulder to cry on. Life had suddenly gone topsy-turvy and it was all down to Blaine. She didn't know if she wanted to thank him or blame him.

The next morning Maisie awoke to the sweet scent of honeysuckle and jasmine drifting in through the open window, and after she had padded across the room and peered out she saw the whole of the back of the house was engulfed in the rich-smelling flowers. 'What a gorgeous place.' She breathed the words out into the perfumed air and felt like pinching herself to make sure it was all real. This time yesterday she had been in a grotty little bedsit in London; today she was in another world.

After a quick shower she pulled on a pair of jeans and a light top, looped her hair into a high ponytail and was downstairs and in the breakfast room by ten to six. It was only as she was greeted by Liliana and led to the table where two places were set that she realised she might have committed her first *faux pas*. It was clear Liliana did not eat with the family and she had all but invited herself to share breakfast with Blaine's mother. She was employed to do a job the same as the housekeeper. Why hadn't she considered she might eat separately with Liliana the night before?

When Jenny joined her a moment later Maisie knew she had to set the record straight immediately. 'I'm so sorry.' She stared at Blaine's mother in an agony of embarrassment. 'I should have realised I wouldn't eat in here with you. I just wasn't thinking last night.'

'Oh, Maisie.' Jenny's hand had gone to her breast. 'I thought you were going to say you'd changed your mind and wanted to go home. Of *course* you will eat with me and Guiseppe when he comes home. We've been trying to persuade Liliana to sit with us for thirty-five years, but she's adamantly stuck in the old ways and won't budge from her kitchen.'

Jenny plumped herself down at the table, her voice soft when she added, 'For the first time in ages I slept well last night. I'm sure it was because my mind was at rest about things here and I knew I could concentrate on Guiseppe without having to dash back and forth from the hospital.'

Maisie smiled. Blaine's mother was a darling.

The two women talked through everything they needed to while they ate, and then Maisie and Liliana waved Jenny off and went back into the house, Liliana to see to her kitchen and housework, Maisie to see to the indoor pets and then the horses. Jenny had promised she would ring as soon as she knew Guiseppe was all right but it was almost evening before the call came.

Liliana answered the telephone and when after a moment or two the elderly housekeeper burst into tears, Maisie stared at her, horrified. Liliana passed her the phone before throwing her apron over her head and rocking herself to and fro. 'Hallo?' Maisie didn't know what to say. 'Is that you, Jenny?'

'It's Blaine.' The deep rich voice was dry. 'My father is

doing very well after what turned out to be a bigger operation than they'd thought. I think you need to make Liliana a
cup of coffee with something strong in it.'

'I'll do that.' Maisie was so relieved her legs felt weak.
'I'm so pleased, Blaine. Give your mother and Roberto my
best wishes.'

'How are you coping that end? Any problems?'

Maisie thought of the frenzied pace of the veterinary
practice where she had worked and the hundred and one jobs,
all urgent, which would pile up the minute her back was
turned. Being here in Italy was a holiday in every sense of
the word. 'Everything's fine,' she said reassuringly. 'Tell your
mother the children are all fed and watered and the dogs had
a lovely long walk this afternoon.'

'You took all seven out?' he asked incredulously.

It felt good to have surprised him. 'Of course,' she said
airily. 'They were as good as gold.'

'Even Humphrey?'

'Especially Humphrey,' she said firmly. The little mongrel
was already her favourite. 'He's a perfect angel once you understand him.'

She thought she heard a slight groan before he said, 'I feel
like I'm talking to my mother.'

Well, that wasn't very nice. 'Goodnight, Blaine,' she
said evenly.

'Goodnight, *mia piccola*.'

His voice had been very soft and Maisie hesitated a
moment before she replaced the receiver. She glanced at
Liliana, who had stopped crying long enough to wipe her eyes
with her apron. 'Come on,' she said quietly. 'Blaine says
you've got to have a cup of coffee with a kick in it.'

'*Scusi?* A kick?'

'A spot of brandy,' Maisie clarified. 'And, before you say no, I'm going to make one for myself too.'

Somehow, though, she felt it was going to take more than the odd measure of brandy to help her deal with her increasingly disturbing feelings about life in general and Blaine in particular over the next weeks.

The fact that Liliana allowed her to make the coffee told Maisie the little elderly woman was even more shaken up than she appeared. It had only taken Maisie an hour or two to understand that the kitchen was utterly and totally Liliana's domain; even Blaine's mother had tiptoed about in it that morning before she had left the house. But Liliana was a softie under her capable and somewhat gruff exterior, Maisie thought, as she handed the older woman her coffee, which had a double shot of brandy in it. She had obviously been worried to death about Guiseppe and had been hiding her concern most of the time; hence the reaction when she'd learnt he was going to be all right.

Liliana said much the same as they sipped their coffee together on the veranda, Maisie digging into a batch of the wonderful sticky sugary pastries Liliana had made earlier that day. 'I needed to be strong for Jennifer,' Liliana explained as they looked out over the warm summer evening, the heady smell of honeysuckle and jasmine and climbing roses heavy in the slumbering air. 'You understand? To be her, how do you say it, her rock?'

Maisie nodded. 'Yes, I understand,' she said, wondering what magic Liliana used to make such incredible melting pastry.

'She is a good woman, and brave, but she has had so much to contend with.'

Maisie nodded again. It was clear Liliana needed to talk and to have her listen, and with the plate of pastries within reach she had no argument with that. The dogs were all spread out around their feet, Humphrey in prime position on her foot as usual, waiting for any crumbs that might fall. Like the cats, they knew enough to keep very quiet and still around Liliana unless they wanted to be shooed off.

'It hit both of them very hard, the trouble with Blaine. He tried to shield his mother, of course, but…' Liliana shrugged, her thin black-clad shoulders eloquent.

Maisie pricked up her ears. Liliana obviously thought that as a friend of the family—as she had been described, apparently—she knew more than she did. She wondered if she ought to warn Liliana that she didn't know anything about Blaine—it would be the right thing to do. Morality warred with curiosity. No contest. Maisie bit into another pastry and looked sympathetic.

'Not that I thought Francesca was right for him.' Liliana had lowered her voice as though she thought if she spoke too loudly it would reach Blaine's ears umpteen miles away. 'She was a sweet girl, of course, well brought up, but just because the pair were childhood sweethearts it does not follow that all will be well. But Jennifer and Guiseppe being Francesca's godparents, and the two families such friends…' She sighed. 'My poor Blaine. Tragic.'

She took another sip of coffee, her face contemplative, and Maisie wanted to snatch the cup away from Liliana's lips. *Don't stop. Go on.* But it appeared Liliana had finished. She drained her coffee and stood up, her manner suddenly brisk. 'I shall go to early mass tomorrow and give thanks to the Holy Mother,' she announced with dramatic intensity. 'She has spared my family more pain.' And with that she disappeared into the house.

Maisie licked her fingers. She was tempted to follow

Liliana and see if she would say more; the brandy had obviously loosened the old woman's tongue. But then that would be somewhat sly and underhand, she admitted, refusing to acknowledge the little voice that said she had been less than honest in letting Liliana rattle on in the first place.

She had just *listened*, she told herself. Had provided a sympathetic ear at a time when Liliana needed one. That was all. She frowned to herself. And really she knew little more than she had initially, except that Blaine's old love had been Italian and dearly loved by his parents by all accounts.

Francesca. Beautiful name. Probably beautiful woman. Long black hair, hauntingly lovely face, stunning figure. Model-thin.

There were two pastries left on the plate and Maisie divided them between the ecstatic dogs, the three she had already eaten now screaming their calories in her head. As Humphrey stood guard over the last of the crumbs on the floor, fur bristling as he almost choked trying to lick up every morsel before any of the others nosed in, she smoothed her hands over her rounded hips. OK, so she wasn't grossly fat but she would never be a supermodel. She was, as boyfriends in the past had described her, cuddly.

She sighed, staring across the lawned garden directly in front of her to where the two horses were standing in the paddock in the distance under the shade of a big old green oak tree. The sunlight was already dappled; within an hour or two the vivid blue of the sky would begin to mellow and her first full day at the villa would come to an end. She wasn't going to like it when she had to return to England.

The thought brought her out of the doldrums with a jolt. What was the matter with her? she asked herself crossly. She had weeks and weeks to look forward to in this glorious place; why on earth was she whining about having to go back home now?

It was the emotion of the last hour, she decided, rising to her feet and then smiling as the dogs rose expectantly, tails wagging and tongues lolling. 'Just a walk down to see your slightly bigger friends then,' she told them, picking up a couple of apples for the two horses from a bowl on one of the small tables on the veranda.

As she stepped out of the shade into the blaze of late afternoon sunshine she lifted her head to the heat. The foreign brightness to the quality of the light and the overall intensity of colour about her made her feel alive from the top of her head to the tips of her toes. She was going to stop analysing everything, she told herself firmly. From now on she would just take each day as it came. No more heart-searching. No more regrets. Blaine was right. Jeff would never have suited her in the long run, nor she him. But she was free, free and footloose and independent. Mistress of her own destiny and answerable to no one. Anticipation and excitement flooded her blood.

This wonderful crazy feeling might not last, she thought as she walked down towards the paddock, the dogs sniffing and bounding and tumbling each other over. But it was enough that she had felt it today because now she knew she would feel it again. Her life wasn't over because Jeff didn't want her—far from it. She had got herself into a tangle of maudlin self-pity in England; she had needed a complete change of scene to break the cycle.

As the two horses came ambling over to her when she reached the fence of the paddock, their large expressive eyes fixed on the apples in her hands, she laughed out loud. 'Cupboard loves.' She let their velvet nuzzles nose the food out of her hands.

She would thank Blaine when she saw him next, she decided as the horses crunched their titbits. She would tell him it had been the right decision for her to come here, that she was grateful to him for suggesting it.

She pictured the long lean length of him in her mind as she stood on the bottom rung of the fence, her hair wafting about her face in the hot breeze. The striking, almost luminescent black-lashed eyes, the firm hard mouth, chiselled cheekbones, strong jaw. His body was superb but aggressively masculine, virile, unyielding. He would make love all night and still want more. The core of her sexuality stirred, shocking her as an aching thrill of pleasure took hold.

Colour flooded her cheeks and she jumped down from the fence, amazed at herself. Blaine Morosini wasn't her type, not at all, so why did she feel as though he had just caressed her in the most intimate place? It was ridiculous, nonsensical, but true nonetheless. She had never felt like this before, even when Jeff was kissing her and touching her, so how could Blaine produce such sensual feelings when he wasn't even here?

Rebound. She seized the word and held on to it like a lifeline. That was all this was. For some reason her body had reacted to Blaine from the first time she had seen him; it was a relief to admit it to herself at last. He was so very different, the opposite in fact, to the sort of male she usually liked and so, hurt and upset as she had been over Jeff, she had swung to the opposite end of the scale. Classic rebound scenario. Didn't mean a thing. And she had known a man like Blaine couldn't possibly be interested in someone like her so her sub-conscious had told her she was safe.

'Whew.' She sighed loudly. What a relief. She wasn't going round the bend after all. Her body was going a bit haywire, admittedly, but she could control that. She wasn't a nymphomaniac, far from it. She dared to bet there weren't too many twenty-eight-year-old virgins around these days.

A whine at her feet brought her eyes down to Humphrey, who clearly thought he was due a bit of attention. She smiled, kneeling down and fussing the little animal, who promptly rolled over on his back in submissive adoration. 'You're more lucky than you know,' she murmured, rubbing the jumbo size ears which felt like velvet. 'No complicated relationships or muddled thoughts for you. You see, you like, you conquer. If the lady is willing, of course. If not, you sail off looking for the next lucky female. No broken heart or hurt feelings. Totally sensible.'

Humphrey seemed to laugh at her, tongue lolling and eyes bright. She fussed him a little more and then stood up and together, the rest of the dogs following, they walked back towards the house.

CHAPTER FIVE

THE following day was a peaceful one. Maisie mucked out the stables and, once they were fresh and sweet-smelling, exercised Iorwerth, the stallion. Before she had left, Jenny had told her the name was Welsh and meant Lord of worth; Iola, the mare's name, being the feminine diminutive. 'My father was Welsh,' Jenny had explained when Maisie had asked how the names had come to be chosen. 'Although his parents immigrated to America when he was only four years old, he was careful not to lose knowledge of the language, and all the horses on our ranch had Welsh names. I suppose I just carried on the tradition here.'

Italian, American, Welsh—Blaine certainly had a cocktail of blood flowing in his veins, Maisie thought as she walked back to the house after taking the dogs for another long walk in the afternoon. Perhaps that was why he was so…unusual? The word mocked her with its meekness.

She felt sticky and hot as she ladled out the dog and cat food into the respective bowls, which she then placed on the veranda at the back of the house. It was the only place in the whole of the villa that Liliana allowed the animals to eat and drink, but as Maisie stood watching the rows of dishes—red ones for the dogs and white for the cats, with Leonardo, the

Labrador, having his own special black one because he was on a prescribed diet for diabetes—and the little heads all avidly eating, she reflected that they didn't do too badly. Plenty of good food, canine and feline company, lovely surroundings, all their needs catered for—if she came back as an animal she'd love it to be a cat or a dog under Jenny's care!

After washing the bowls thoroughly she put them away and went upstairs to her room to shower and change before dinner. Dumping her jeans and shirt—which still smelt vaguely of horse—in the linen basket in a corner of her bathroom, she stepped under the cool cleansing flow of water in the shower. It was heavenly. Although she had used lashings of sun-lotion and had been careful not to burn, her skin had felt hot and irritated by the end of the day. The velvet-soft water was just what she needed. After standing for some minutes just letting the water take all the aches and pains of a physically tiring day out of her limbs, she washed her hair before wrapping a bath sheet round her and walking through to the bedroom.

She creamed her face and body, noticing the slight golden tint to her skin with some delight, and then dried her hair, letting it fall in soft waves about her shoulders. She had insisted she wanted to eat with Liliana in the kitchen while Jenny was away and now she slipped on a light linen shift dress without bothering with any make-up or jewellery. No need to dress up, she told herself as she yawned at her reflection in the mirror. She was so tired that she doubted she'd last till pudding anyway.

As she walked downstairs she noticed Liliana exiting the formal dining room, however. 'Liliana?' She frowned at the housekeeper. 'I thought I was eating in the kitchen with you?'

'My fault, I'm afraid.' As Blaine appeared in the doorway

of the sitting room, a glass of wine in his hand, Maisie felt her heart actually jump. 'I said we'd all sit in the kitchen but Liliana wouldn't have it, neither will she join us. Stubborn.' His eyes left Maisie as he smiled at the little housekeeper, and Maisie used the time to compose herself and catch her breath. By the time she joined him in the hall she hoped the hot flood of colour she knew had stained her cheeks bright red had died down somewhat.

'I didn't know you were eating here tonight,' she managed quite casually as she followed him into the sitting room, accepting the glass of red wine he handed her in the next moment with a nod of thanks.

'Neither did I.' He smiled and her heart did that funny little hop thing again. 'I came by mainly to reassure Liliana that my father is definitely holding his own and she insisted I stay for dinner. I think she feels I don't cook for myself well enough.'

He came by to reassure Liliana. Maisie took a big sip of wine, hoping it would begin to soothe her frazzled nerve-endings by the time she had to sit facing him over the dining table. The two of them. By themselves. 'And do you?' she said as the wine warmed the little cold bit in her stomach his words about Liliana had caused. 'Cook for yourself, I mean?'

'Of course; I'm Italian.' He sat down on one of the sofas, one knee over the other and one arm along the back of the seat as he surveyed her with laughing eyes. 'We're all wonderful chefs from birth; didn't you know?'

She tried to enter into the spirit of the thing but it was hard because he looked so darn fanciable. Now she had acknowledged this strange effect he had on her, it seemed to have multiplied alarmingly and she had goose-pimples on her goose-pimples. 'Do you even do barbecues?' she asked, smiling back. And then hoped he didn't think she was poking fun at poor Roberto.

'Now and again, but I prefer to think of them as meals eaten alfresco rather than your English version of taking a piece of unprepared meat and cooking it until it resembles coal.'

'Excuse me!' She couldn't work out if he was teasing her or not but she wasn't going to let him get away with that. 'I know loads of English people who marinate their meat beforehand and produce wonderful results.'

'This is good.' He nodded gravely. 'You are restoring my faith in the nation's culinary expertise after my experience at Roberto's.'

'Ah, but Roberto is Italian,' Maisie pointed out triumphantly. 'So, if you're basing your judgement of our barbecues on him, that's flawed reasoning. It should be me that's saying I have my doubts about Italian barbecues, surely? Not that I think Jackie's father is a bad cook, far from it,' she added hastily. 'He's great, as it happens.'

'But not at the English barbecue.' His face was unsmiling but the greeny-blue eyes were wicked.

'Not at *any* barbecue,' she corrected severely, trying to ignore how sexy he looked and how the fluttering action in the pit of her stomach was gathering steam.

'Right. Point taken.'

'Anyway, how is your father, exactly?' said Maisie. 'You mentioned it was a bigger operation than expected.'

Blaine nodded. 'He was lucky they brought the operation forward,' he said quietly. 'Too many years of rich eating and no exercise had clogged up his veins, arteries, valves.' He shook his head. 'I'd been telling him for years to get checked out. Hell, he has enough money to get the best medical care for the rest of his life and not worry about it. To cut a long story short, the blood circulation to and from the heart had clogged up to the point where it had almost stopped. He could have had a major heart attack at any moment. But perhaps this was meant to reunite my father and Roberto? Who knows? Certainly, hearing them talk before the operation, I realised for the first time my father was as much to blame for the quarrel as Roberto. More so, probably.'

Maisie nodded, relieved he had come to that conclusion.

'And you? Can you manage the animals without assistance?'

'There's not really anything to manage. To be honest, I feel an absolute fraud that I'm being paid for this. I would much prefer we forget about that. Your mother has paid for my tickets and everything's settled in England; this is like a holiday to me.'

He frowned. 'We had an arrangement, did we not?'

'But that was before I came here, before I met your mother and everything. I don't want any more money.'

The beautiful eyes had narrowed on her face and Maisie was finding it extremely uncomfortable. If she had known he was going to be here she would have made a little effort—put on some mascara at least. It didn't help that he was as immaculately turned out as usual and looked good enough to eat. He was wearing a thin pale coffee-coloured shirt today and she could see a dark shadow over his chest denoting black body hair. It did something peculiar to her own body she could well have done without with that piercing gaze fixed on her.

'You are a very unusual young woman. I thought this when we first met, but on further acquaintance I find you more so.'

His voice had been soft but Maisie stared at him warily. Unusual as in nice, or unusual as in weird? she wanted to ask. She didn't, though—he might give the wrong answer.

'And you do not realise this, do you? You do not understand your own worth. This, of course, is part of your charm but also your undoing, I feel.'

Maisie's train of thought had become so tangled she didn't know what to say. She stared at him dumbly as he stood up and came to kneel in front of her, his eyes on a level with her wide brown ones.

'It is this quality in you that draws weak characters like this Jeff person to your strength. Do you know what I mean?'

Maisie shook her head. At this moment she wasn't even sure who Jeff was, not with Blaine so close she could smell that delicious aftershave again, and, very faintly, hospitals.

Blaine smiled, a sexy quirk of his slightly uneven mouth. It was a fabulous mouth, Maisie thought feverishly. Magnificent. It was coming closer...

She gave herself up to the utterly mindless thrill of his kiss. His mouth was firm and warm and he kissed her slowly and deeply, taking his time. It was the sort of kiss she had dreamed about when she was a spotty schoolgirl, before she had grown up and realised you couldn't believe everything you read in lurid novels under the bedclothes by the light of a torch.

It didn't last long enough. When he drew away and rose to his feet Maisie almost cried out in protest, before, that was, she realised he must have heard Liliana's heels clicking on the wooden floor of the hall. The next second the housekeeper's head popped round the sitting room door. 'Dinner is ready,' she said brightly, her face portraying the fact that whatever reassurance Blaine had given her about his father had worked. 'And it is your favourite,' she added to Blaine. 'You must have known I was making *carpaccio* tonight, *sì*?'

'Liliana, I always live in the hope you are making *carpaccio*,' Blaine said lazily.

Maisie stared at him. He was quite unaffected by a kiss that had rocked her down to her toes. How could he just stand there like that, all relaxed and smiling?

When he offered her his hand in the next moment she ignored it, standing up and preceding him out of the room as she said to Liliana, 'I hope you've saved enough for yourself?'

Liliana made a very Italian sound, midway between a clicking of the tongue and a grunt in the back of her throat. '*Sì, sì*,' she said, clearly impatient. 'Now come and eat.'

Blaine had brought the bottle of wine through with him but, although he poured her another glass, Maisie noticed he only helped himself to the jug of water on the table. She felt acutely ill at ease as she sat at the vast dining table, which Liliana had laid with two places, one at the head facing the door and the other to its left. She would have much preferred the less formal breakfast room but she knew Liliana would have been horrified if she had even suggested such a thing. The Italian housekeeper was traditional to her last breath. But the heavy silver cutlery, fine linen napkins and beautifully set table complete with a small bowl of fresh flowers all added to her embarrassment. This felt too much like a date.

The *carpaccio*—a dish of paper-thin slices of fillet steak garnished with fresh egg mayonnaise and finely slivered parmesan—was delicious, as were the accompanying vegetables, but Maisie was finding it difficult to eat. She was acutely aware of Liliana standing at Blaine's elbow, watching him with a benign smile on her face as he took his first couple of mouthfuls.

'Excellent.' He smacked his lips as he turned to the little housekeeper. 'No one makes *carpaccio* like you, Liliana. You truly have the touch of an angel.'

Liliana smiled a satisfied smile, practically purring like a cat as she left the room.

'A little over the top, don't you think? The touch of an angel?' Maisie didn't know why she was being bitchy, but his complete refusal to be stirred by that mind-boggling kiss had something to do with it.

Blaine paused in his eating, taking a sip of the iced water before he said quietly, 'When Liliana first came to work for my parents in the months before I was born she was recovering from a mental breakdown. It was the result of watching her husband and six children die in a fire caused by the atrocious electrical wiring in the slums where they lived in Naples. It took a long while for her to become the woman you see now, and beneath the black mourning clothes she wears my mother informs me she is heavily scarred from her attempts to rescue her family from the flames. She was returning from her night cleaning job when the accident happened. She has always been completely devoted to my parents and to me. Angel is not too high a praise, I think.'

Maisie swallowed the lump in her throat; she had never felt such a worm in the whole of her life. 'I'm sorry.' She blinked hard. 'I always did have a big mouth.'

Blaine gave the flicker of a smile. 'It is a beautiful mouth and just the right size,' he said softly, his eyes touching her in such a way that she felt weak.

She stared at him. She didn't understand what was happening to her and if it was anyone else explaining to her how they felt, she would tell them to take a long cold shower and act their age. Perhaps that was the trouble? she thought in the next moment. She was twenty-eight years of age and she had never been bedded. Maybe that was what this was all about?

She tore her gaze away from his and gulped at her wine. 'Liliana's a love, I can see that,' she said when she came up for air. 'And this *does* have the touch of heaven about it.' She ate a mouthful of food and closed her eyes in appreciation. When she opened them again his face was an inch from hers and he wasn't smiling any more.

'Poor mixed up little girl,' he said, very softly. 'Forget him. He isn't worth it.'

She didn't like to tell him he was on the wrong lines if he was talking about Jeff. She exhaled slowly. She wanted him to kiss her again, so badly it actually hurt. Which meant she had to be the most flighty female in the world, didn't it? She had only been an ex-fiancée for a few weeks; it wasn't even decent to start fancying another male so fast. And as she would have sworn on oath a week or two ago that it would take months, if not years, to get over Jeff, it was also a bit scary too. She swallowed hard. 'Your *carpaccio* is getting cold.'

This time his warm mouth just skimmed her lips before he settled back in his seat. 'We will talk of other things,' he declared firmly. 'Your childhood. Tell me about that. Were you a happy child?'

Actually, for most of the time she had been horrendously miserable. Her face must have told him something because his expression changed. 'Not a good subject? Then that can wait. For now I will tell you about my childhood, *sì*? Which *was* happy. And later we will have coffee on the veranda where it is dark and easier to talk and you can tell me about your childhood.'

She didn't argue. She couldn't. The dark and easier to talk bit had seen to that.

By the time they walked out on to the veranda Maisie knew a lot more about Blaine Morosini, but nothing which told her about the man, only the child he had been. She knew he had swum every day with his friends as a child on Marina Piccola's beach, which had involved a descent of two hundred steps; that he'd often gone out in a fishing boat with a pal whose father was a fisherman and that the fish they had caught had been baked over an open fire in a small bay only the locals knew about. He'd had his own chestnut mare, which had since died of old age, had learnt the piano and classical guitar and was a black belt in judo. Holidaying abroad with his parents meant he'd seen more countries than she'd had hot dinners, and he spoke several languages. He had been free and happy and had had everything a child could want. But he hadn't mentioned Francesca who, according to Liliana, had been his childhood sweetheart and therefore part of his life at that time. Neither had he spoken of his years since leaving university, when he had taken over the family business.

Maisie sat down in one of the big wicker chairs on the veranda, and once Liliana had bustled away after bringing the coffee she tried to relax. The shadows helped. Blaine had told Liliana not to switch the veranda and garden lights on so the warm darkness all around them was sympathetic to her nerves, which felt as tight as piano wire. She didn't feel she could refuse to talk about her childhood after he had been so eloquent about his, but she intended to keep it short.

With that in mind, she said, 'You were very fortunate to be born here. I lived in London from the age of two when my parents moved there from Sheffield. They moved because of my father's job but my mother never really liked London. It…it wasn't a happy marriage. My father left when I was eight and went to America. I missed him very much.'

'Do you still see him?' Blaine asked softly.

'He died when I was nine years old. An accident.'

'And your mother?'

'We don't get on; we never have. I'm too much like my father, I think.'

'Then your father must have been a warm and generous man.'

She wished he wouldn't say things like that. It probably meant nothing to him but it made her feel…odd. She shrugged. 'He left us. That was hard to take. And when he went my mother got rid of our dog and two cats because my father had loved them. I loved them too but that didn't seem to matter. I think from that time on I never felt the same about her again.'

She hadn't meant to say all that. Maisie reached for her coffee but, as she did so, Blaine's hand closed over hers. 'I'm sorry,' he said quietly. 'You have had a tough deal.'

Maisie's throat tightened. He had said that as though he meant it. She knew she shouldn't have agreed to come and sit in this warm perfumed velvety darkness and talk about things that were best left buried. She probably shouldn't have agreed to come to Italy, if it came to that. Perhaps she was losing her mind? And he still hadn't mentioned Francesca; all he'd done was to rave about his childhood. Not exactly fair, however you looked at it. Still, she couldn't force him to come clean.

She slid her hand from under his and this time managed to reach her cup and saucer. Taking a long gulp at the fragrant liquid, she found it was scalding hot and winced as she swallowed. Great, now she was minus the roof of her mouth as well as her mind.

The dogs had been lying snoozing on the veranda when they had walked out of the house; now she felt Humphrey edge forward and position himself on her foot. Glad of the diversion, she bent forward and stroked the large silky ears. 'Missing your mum?' she said softly. 'She'll be back soon.'

'I had better be going.' Blaine finished his coffee and rose to his feet and Maisie stood up too. She wondered if he would try and kiss her again or suggest they go out somewhere over the next few days.

He didn't. 'Goodnight, Maisie,' he said quietly. 'Any problems of any kind, phone me. Liliana has my home and work numbers.'

She nodded briskly. 'OK, but I'm sure everything will be just fine.'

Did he expect her to walk through the house with him and wave him off? Or would that seem presumptuous?

Liliana settled this in the next moment as she reappeared, saying, 'You are not leaving already, Blaine? I came to see if you would like a liqueur with your coffee?'

'I have an early start tomorrow morning.' He took Liliana's arm as he spoke and the two of them disappeared into the house, leaving Maisie standing on the veranda. She wasn't sure if she was supposed to follow them, but she didn't. She sat down instead, pouring herself another coffee and drinking it slowly with Humphrey back on her foot as she heard them talking in Italian in the hall. After a while she heard a car start at the front of the house and a few moments later Liliana joined her.

'Blaine has suggested he take me to see Guiseppe in a day or two if you feel confident to look after everything here for a few hours?' Liliana said happily.

'Of course, that'll be fine.'

'He is a good boy.' Liliana didn't seem to expect a comment from her as she bustled about clearing the tray and Maisie was glad of this because she couldn't think of one.

Later, up in her room, Maisie sat for a long time by the open window, her brow wrinkled and her thoughts going back and forth until she gave herself a headache. Why had he kissed her? And, more to the point, after he had why hadn't he come back for more? Even *more* to the point than that though, why had she longed for a repeat performance with every cell of her body?

Dangerous, dangerous man. She gave a mental nod to the declaration. And danger was the last thing she needed in her life after all the anguish of the last weeks. She was glad he hadn't tried to kiss her again or suggest a date or anything like that. She ignored the cold little lump in the pit of her stomach as she stood up and began undressing. And she would make sure she stayed out of his way as much as possible while she was in Italy. No more cosy chats over dinner, no more silly fancies and muddled thoughts.

She didn't bother to wash, just brushing her teeth and pulling on her nightie before she climbed into bed. Once under the cool cotton sheet she shut her eyes determinedly. She was *not* going to lie awake half the night doing endless post-mortems about the evening in her mind. She had to be up at the crack of dawn to see to the horses and the rest of the animals. Blaine Morosini was not part of her life. He never could or would be. And she didn't want him to be.

She turned over, burying her face in the soft plump pillow, but, much to her irritation, it was still a long time before she eventually fell asleep.

CHAPTER SIX

THE next week or so was fairly uneventful. Blaine had fallen into the habit of dropping by each night to give Liliana a report on Guiseppe, but apart from that first evening he wouldn't be pressed to stay for dinner. He stayed for a coffee with the two women but the conversation was always light and encouraging on his part; he often made Liliana smile by relating some funny incident that had occurred either at the hospital or during his day at work.

There were no more long looks and certainly no more kisses; in fact, Maisie thought that if she hadn't been absolutely certain of the events that night when they had shared dinner together, she would have begun to think that she had imagined the whole thing. But she hadn't. And for that reason she let Blaine and Liliana do most of the talking while she sat quietly listening to them. Actually, it was surprising what she learnt about Blaine this way, she told herself as she sat on the veranda one night when she had been in Italy nine days, the dogs spread out about her feet.

She now knew he was a man who only needed three or four hours' sleep a night. She realised this when it had transpired he left his house every morning at five o'clock to fit in a full day's work before, more often than not, calling in at the hospital to see his father before he came back to Sorrento. She also knew he hadn't got a girlfriend and hadn't dated for some time. This had been revealed during one conversation when Liliana had scolded him for being a workaholic.

'I tell him he should have a little fun,' the housekeeper had said in an aside to Maisie. 'But it is all work, work, work. This is not good for a man, I think.'

Blaine had changed the conversation very firmly at this point and Maisie had wondered if it was because he had been worried Liliana might bring up the past and the reason he made work his life these days. Was it to do with Francesca? She rather thought it might be. But of course it was none of her business—not that that didn't stop her thinking about it most of the time.

It didn't help that Liliana had buttoned up about Blaine's past love life either. Maisie was almost certain he'd warned the housekeeper to say nothing to her. She could be being paranoid here, but she didn't think so. And she hadn't imagined the reserve that was in his manner towards her now either. Obviously that kiss had been a complete nonentity as far as he was concerned. Which was fine, just fine, because she wasn't on for a repeat either. It just rankled that she was clearly such a bad kisser that she'd put him off so completely, that was all. She didn't have bad breath or buck teeth or weepy sores, so what was the problem?

Blaine had taken Liliana to see Guiseppe on two occasions now and each time Maisie had made sure she was in bed when he'd returned the housekeeper to the villa late at night. She knew he always came in and had a nightcap with Liliana but she wasn't about to hang around like little orphan Annie. Tonight was the third time and as Maisie finished her coffee she rose to her feet, the dogs all jumping up too. They knew the routine now. After-dinner snooze on the veranda and then this new human always walked down to the paddock before she went to bed.

Maisie put the stable lights on when she reached the paddock. She had brought both horses into the stables from the paddock earlier because Iola hadn't seemed quite right all day and she wondered if the mare was close to her time. She had telephoned Jenny's vet for advice but he'd been unconcerned, merely telling her to keep an eye on the mare and call him if there was a problem. But Iola was young and healthy, he'd said, and he would expect the foaling to take place without him having to attend. Which was all very well in the normal run of things, Maisie thought, but when she was in sole charge of the beautiful and very expensive animal…

The stables were relatively new and luxurious by any standards; apparently the old ones had been knocked down and replaced a couple of years ago. Maisie had put the mare in one of the well-lit loose boxes with an empty one between her and Iorwerth, and she was glad of this when she saw the graceful animal straining and paddling her limbs. She had attended several foalings in her days as a veterinary nurse and she sensed immediately that something was wrong.

She ran back to the house and called the vet's number again. The mare's efforts were producing nothing; there were no little hooves protruding from the vulva, which could mean a malpresentation, possibly a breech. This wasn't such a problem in a cow, but the vets she had worked with had always bemoaned the tremendous length of the foal's legs in such cases.

This time when she spoke to Jenny's vet he listened and was at the house within fifteen minutes. By the time Blaine brought Liliana home and came down to the stables, Maisie was doing what she could to assist the vet in what was indeed a breech delivery. She knew as well as he did that foals sometimes didn't survive in such cases and she was praying like mad this wouldn't happen here.

After ascertaining the situation, Blaine stood quietly by and watched proceedings and, for once, tied up in the fight for the foal's life, Maisie was practically oblivious to his presence. It was half an hour before the vet managed to bring the tiny animal's legs round and move it into the correct position for birth and immediately Iola sensed the obstruction was gone. She gave a great heave and the foal shot out on to the thick bed of straw Maisie had prepared, jerking convulsively and very much alive. In the next few moments it was shaking its head and snorting out the placental fluid it had inhaled, Iola seemingly forgetting all her pain and displaying a fond interest in her baby.

'Whew.' Maisie knelt back on the straw and beamed up at the vet. 'Thank you so much, Mr Rossellini.'

'No, thank *you*, *signorina*. Time was of the essence and you did not delay.' He turned to Blaine as he wiped his hands with the towel Maisie had passed him as he added, 'Your mother has much to thank this young lady for. She is a capable young woman.'

'I'm aware of that.' Blaine smiled at her, his eyes warm.

'If ever you want a job, *signorina*, you come and see me, *sì*?' Mr Rossellini bobbed his head at her. 'I mean this.'

'Thank you.' Maisie had been in all kinds of awkward positions as she had helped the vet with the birth and now she found it hard to stand. Iola was nuzzling the foal, clearly delighted with what she'd accomplished, and Maisie stroked the soft muzzle as she murmured, 'You're a clever girl and you have a beautiful baby. Iorwerth is going to be delighted with his son.'

Blaine accompanied Mr Rossellini back to the house and

Maisie let the two men go, content to stay with the new mother and her foal for a while. Iorwerth had been stamping about his box, clearly disturbed, but like the intuitive beast he was he now seemed to know all was well and was blowing gently down his nose. Maisie went over and talked to him for a while, reassuring him, before she returned to Iola and her baby. She stood leaning against the box, captivated by the sight of the mother and foal, the fragrance of the straw and the soft sounds from the horses magical after all the panic and worry of the last hour or so.

How long she stood there she didn't know, but when she felt a pair of strong hands on her shoulders and Blaine's voice in her ear murmuring, 'There's not a more beautiful sight, is there?' she knew she'd been expecting he would return. 'Mr Rossellini is full of admiration for your ability,' he continued, 'as am I. You were so calm and capable.'

He wouldn't think she was calm if he knew how her heart was beating like a tom-tom against her ribs. 'It's my job.' She tried to ignore the tingles radiating down from her shoulders. 'It's what I've been trained for.'

'Still…' He turned her round, tilting her chin. 'You were perfect. You *are* perfect.'

If she had just ducked away at that point, made some excuse, anything, she might still have been all right. As it was, she waited for his kiss and when it came she kissed him back. There were a hundred reasons not to and she didn't care about any of them.

They stood locked together, swaying slightly, and as she felt the heady rush of sensation sending needles of pleasure into every nerve and sinew, she wondered what he had that made him so darn *good* at this. But it didn't matter what it was; it was enough that he was kissing her.

Blaine was breathing hard as his mouth continued to move on hers, tasting her, fuelling and feeding on the reaction he was causing. His hands moved up and down her body and she trembled at his touch, shifting in his arms so that she could lift her hands to his shoulders and press more closely against the long hard length of him.

She could feel his heart pounding against his chest like a sledgehammer and it was incredibly exhilarating to know she could arouse such desire in him. His thighs were hard against hers as he moved her against the stable wall, his kiss deepening into what was almost a consummation in itself as his tongue took vanquished territory.

It was Liliana's voice that broke into the madness which had taken hold, but even as it registered and she felt him stiffen it was still another sweet moment or two before he raised his head and drew away. She felt his going in every nerve in her body. 'Liliana,' he muttered hoarsely. 'She's fixing sandwiches and a hot drink.'

'Right.' She knew her voice was as bemused as his. 'We'd better go then.'

'Maisie…' Her name was a caress on his tongue. 'You are driving me mad. I sit at my desk and I see you in front of me, I talk to my staff and your face is there. What have you done to me?'

'I don't know.' She shivered, under such a strong spell of sensual desire all self-protection had broken down. 'But, whatever it is, I feel the same.'

The last was almost in the form of a plaintive protest and whether it was that which gave him the strength to straighten and put a few inches between them she didn't know. He stared at her, his eyes glittering and almost opaque in the strong lights in the stable as he said, 'This is wrong. I am taking advantage of you when you are at your most vulnerable. This man, your fiancé, has hurt you and taken away your self-esteem. You need to prove to yourself that you are still desirable.'

No, no that wasn't it. Jeff was such a wash-out, so unimportant right at this moment that he didn't even begin to come into the equation. She wondered how she could say that without sounding as if she was begging him to make love to her.

'Blaine—'

'I am not the man you think I am, *mia piccola*. You are looking for a white knight and I am not he. I cannot give you what you want.'

'You can.' Oh, he could, he *could*. And who needed a white knight anyway?

'Maisie—' he took a step backwards away from her as Liliana's voice called again and, much as Maisie liked the little housekeeper, she could have throttled her right at this moment '—believe me. This will only end badly.'

She didn't care. She really, *really* didn't care. 'It won't.'

'There are things you don't know.'

'So tell me.' She faced him, hands on hips, and Iola snorted from her box as though to say she was with her, body and soul. Women together and all that. 'Tell me what I don't know.'

Liliana's voice was closer this time and then the housekeeper was at the stable doors. 'How is the horse?' Liliana cast a wary eye at Iola. 'There are no problems?'

'No, everything's fine.' Maisie spoke into the void when it appeared Blaine wasn't going to. 'I was just settling her down, that's all.'

Liliana smiled. 'This will be a nice homecoming gift, *sì*? Jennifer and Guiseppe will be pleased. New life is a good omen.'

Maisie smiled, but she looked straight at Blaine as she said,

'I agree, Liliana. New life is a very good omen. A reminder that the past is gone and the future is bright.'

'The animal is all right to be left, *sì*?' Again Liliana cast a wary glance at Iola. Her affinity with the horses was so non-existent it was clear she was worried that Iola could suddenly barge out of the loose box and go berserk. When Maisie nodded she added, 'Come and have a hot drink now. You must be exhausted.'

'Exhilarated, actually,' Maisie said as she followed Liliana out into the warm night. She was aware of Blaine at the side of her with every fibre of her being although she didn't glance at him as they walked back to the house, but her lips were aching and full as a result of his kisses and her body was burning.

Had he said what he'd said purely because he was worried this was all happening too fast for her after Jeff? Somehow she didn't think so. There was more, much more. That bit about not being a white knight, for example. Something had happened to him with this Francesca and, frankly, after what had transpired tonight between them, she felt she deserved an explanation. Her chin lifted. However difficult it might be for him. Everyone had broken love affairs, didn't they? Everyone got let down at some time in their lives. If ever anyone had the T-shirt for that, she had. Two, in fact.

They drank the coffee and ate the sandwiches sitting in the kitchen and for once Liliana didn't protest but chatted away nineteen to the dozen, clearly on a high after her visit to see Guiseppe and Jenny. Maisie was glad of the diversion. Now the initial furore following Blaine's love-making had died down, she was facing the grim reality that she was no further forward than she had been at the beginning of the evening. He was making polite conversation and injecting the odd comment to keep Liliana going but he obviously wanted to be anywhere but here with her. How could he blow so hot and cold? It wasn't fair.

As soon as he had eaten his sandwiches he rose to his feet, his voice pleasant but cool as he said, 'Mother will be thrilled about the foal, Maisie. Thank you again for all you did. I've got a series of meetings over the next few days, so I guess I might not be calling in.'

This last was directed to Liliana but Maisie knew it was meant for her. For a moment her newly found determination faltered and all her self-doubts poured in. Then she mentally slapped herself. She was *not* going to let this…thing between them fizzle and go out like a damp squib without at least demanding some sort of justification for his actions. OK, so her legs didn't go up to her eyeballs and she didn't have a figure to die for, but he couldn't have made love to her like that unless he fancied her. And he had instigated it, not her. And, she thought grimly, his body had stated he wanted her, regardless of what he had said afterwards.

With this in mind she took a deep breath and stared straight at him, her voice casual and just faintly surprised as she said, 'But you'll see Liliana tomorrow when you call to pick me up, won't you? You haven't forgotten you're taking me out to dinner?'

Ball in his court. He could either show her up in front of Liliana and make her look like a cheap liar coming on to him by calling her bluff, or behave like the gentleman she suspected him to be and fall in with what she freely admitted was an outrageous manoeuvre on her part. But only because he had left her with no other option, she told herself desperately when the beautiful eyes narrowed on her pink face. She had to be able to be alone with him and talk properly. That was all she wanted—an explanation. Well, not all perhaps, but it would do for starters.

'Of course.' He had only hesitated for the barest of moments. 'How silly of me.'

She smiled but it was the sort of smile that stuck at the edges. 'I'll see you about seven o'clock as arranged, then?'

He nodded and Maisie wondered if Liliana had noticed the faintly bemused expression on his face. 'Seven o'clock,' he repeated softly.

Liliana clearly hadn't observed a thing; in fact, she was beaming at them. 'You are going out to dinner?' she said with evident satisfaction. 'How nice.'

'Isn't it?' Blaine murmured as he turned away and walked out of the kitchen, calling over his shoulder. 'Mother's probably asleep by now but I'll text her about the foal and no doubt she'll ring before she goes into the hospital tomorrow morning.'

How could she have done that? The second he had left Maisie felt hot all over. What on earth was he thinking? Well, she knew what he was thinking! Pushy female would be the least of it. No man liked to be pursued; they liked to be the pursuer, didn't they? That was what all the magazines said anyway. And if you did pursue them you had to do it in such a way that they either didn't realise or could at least pretend they didn't. Whereas she had been blatantly—she wanted to say upfront but honesty insisted on—brazen. If Liliana hadn't been present she would have groaned out loud.

The housekeeper had just walked back into the kitchen after seeing Blaine out and now she said eagerly, 'So Blaine has invited you to dinner? You did not tell me of this.'

Maisie thought on her feet. 'It was when we were down with the foal,' she said quickly. 'A sort of reward, I think. You know, for calling Mr Rossellini and everything.'

Liliana's face dropped just for a second and then she said,

'No, I do not think it was this. He likes you, I can tell.' Her countenance brightened. 'I am sure of it.'

Maisie wondered what she had started. Carefully she said, 'As a friend, yes.'

'A friend?' Liliana surveyed her with bright worldly eyes. 'Huh! I do not believe in this modern idea of a man and a woman being friends. Not when they are both young and un-attached. It is not possible. There is always the, how do you say, the chemistry between them. *Sì*?'

Oh, help. Maisie shrugged and tried a new tack. 'Blaine's a workaholic; isn't that what you said? That's not conducive to chemistry, surely?'

'Oh, that.' Liliana dismissed her earlier comments with a very Latin lift of her shoulders. 'That is nothing. Not if the right woman comes along.'

'We're only going to dinner, Liliana.'

'*Sì, sì*, I know. But he asked you, did he not? And you accepted.'

Oh, what a tangled web we weave, when first we practise to deceive. Maisie gave up. 'I'm off to bed,' she said quietly. 'It's been a long day.' And it would probably be a long night the way she was feeling, because she had never regretted anything so much in her life and probably wouldn't be able to sleep a wink.

CHAPTER SEVEN

JENNY rang the house at eight o'clock the next morning and enthused for some minutes about Iola's foal. 'I want you to name him,' she told Maisie. 'Blaine said things might have been very different if it wasn't for you and I can never thank you enough. I was sure she wouldn't do anything for a while and that I'd be back. If anything had happened to her…'

'But it didn't,' Maisie said quickly. 'Iola's fine and her baby is just beautiful, Jenny. You'll fall in love when you see him. But I can't name him; that's for you to do.'

'No, no, I insist. Have a think about a name; anything you like. I want you to do it.'

They talked for some more moments before they said goodbye, and once Maisie had put down the telephone she prepared the cat and dog food and took the bowls out to the veranda where her charges were all lined up waiting. She stood gazing out over the garden and paddock as the animals ate, the bright golden sunlight, high blue sky and fresh warm air mocking her sombre mood. She had been down to see the horses first thing before breakfast and the stables had screamed Blaine. Everything screamed Blaine. At some point during the long wakeful night she had conceded she had made a terrible mistake in engineering their date tonight and would have given the world to go back in time and change things. But she couldn't. And it would make things ten times worse to ring up and cancel it now.

She sighed, gathering up the bowls and taking them through to the kitchen where she washed each one under the eagle eye of Liliana, who insisted on separate cloths for the animals' dishes, and that the sink be rinsed with disinfectant once Maisie had finished.

Once that chore was finished she went about grooming the cats and dogs, the dogs submitting to her ministrations with their normal good grace and the cats protesting every inch of the way. Later that morning she introduced Iorwerth to his son and let the three of them into the paddock, standing for some time watching the foal, who was doing splendidly on his still wobbly legs, before taking the dogs for a long walk.

She mucked out the stables in the afternoon and then proceeded to give them an energetic floor to ceiling spring-clean. They didn't really warrant it but she needed to keep working. It was definitely that sort of day. Once they were gleaming and pristine she filled the boxes with sweet-smelling straw, checked the horses had plenty of clean water in the paddock and went back to the house for a coffee with Liliana before taking the dogs out again.

At six o'clock she decided on a long soak in the bath rather than a quick shower, but after only five minutes in the bubble scented water she was out again, unable to lie still and do nothing with her nerves stretched to breaking-point.

She had a nice surprise when she pulled on the dress she had chosen for the evening. It had been a little tight in England; now it was loose in all the right places and fitted her perfectly. And it was a size twelve. All the exercise involved with taking care of the animals was paying off.

She examined her face in the mirror. Her complexion had turned a golden brown and was as clear and smooth as silk. The sun had brought out loads of natural highlights in her hair too, which was as good as an eighty-pound salon visit, and she had definitely lost a little weight from her face because her chin was now one instead of two and she could see evidence of cheekbones for the first time for a while.

Hugely delighted at such a massive bonus, which she'd been totally unaware of until this moment, Maisie decided to go for gold. She was going to spend the next fifty minutes making up her face and doing her hair until she was something to die for, she told herself euphorically. She might not be a black-haired, super-slim, sophisticated Italian beauty but she wouldn't crack any mirrors tonight either after she was done.

By the time she had put hair up and then down twice, she decided she was trying just a bit too hard. Leaving it falling in silky waves to her shoulders, she concentrated on making up her eyes until they looked at least twice as big, her foundation giving her skin a translucent gleam and her lip gloss just the right colour to set off the salmon-pink dress. In England the dress had seemed just a mite daring and she had wondered if she would ever wear it, now it fitted so perfectly she was in no doubt at all. The draped and tied bodice and seductive Empire-line to the skirt was definitely on the flirty side but that was all right, she told herself firmly. She was a girl, wasn't she? She was supposed to have curves that she could show off once in a while.

At five to seven she was ready. Balancing on sandals with wafer-thin heels, she picked up a short-sleeved cotton cardigans and made her way to the kitchen. When Liliana caught sight of her she stopped what she was doing and said something in Italian that—although she didn't have a clue what it meant—made Maisie blush.

'You like it?' she asked to mask her embarrassment, twirling round and then nearly falling over, which rather spoilt the effect.

'*Sì*, I like it.' Liliana smiled. 'And you say there is no chemistry, eh?'

Maisie stared at her, suddenly acutely worried. She didn't want Blaine to think she was throwing herself at him. Should she nip upstairs and change, and perhaps take a little make-up off too?

She didn't have time to even get to the foot of the stairs. She had reached the kitchen door when Blaine's key sounded in the lock and the next moment he had opened the front door. She stood transfixed in the doorway. He had obviously called in on his way home from work because there was a dark stubble on his square chin and he looked tired, rumpled and good enough to eat. Like all her Christmases rolled into one, in fact. She wished.

He walked across to her, a single red rose in his hand. 'You look stunning,' he said softly, 'and I had every intention of doing this properly before a crisis with the air-conditioning at our flagship hotel caused a few problems. It was a case of ringing to say I was going to be horribly late or collecting you en route before I go home to change. I decided on the latter. Right decision?'

Oh, yes. Maisie took the rose and hoped he hadn't noticed her hand was trembling. This way she got to see where he lived *and* had longer with him. 'You can show me a little more of the scenery,' she said evenly, 'so definitely right decision.'

'Good.' He smiled and she noticed the stubble showed he had a tiny cleft in his chin. For such a small thing it had a *huge* effect on her equilibrium.

After saying their goodbyes to Liliana, Blaine walked her out to the Ferrari with a hand at her elbow, and Maisie found she was working on automatic in an effort to ignore the effect he had on her. She had spoken to Jackie earlier in the day— her friend had called her several times while she had been at the villa to see how things were going—and had mentioned they were having dinner together that evening, eliciting a worried response from Blaine's niece.

'Be careful, Maisie.' Jackie had sounded both embarrassed and sincere. 'Mum has told me there's some sort of thing in his past, I don't know what, but it's to do with a woman and it's had a huge effect on him. I'm not saying he's celibate but he never gets emotionally involved, you know? And you don't want anyone with baggage.'

She had fobbed Jackie off with some light comment about this meal being a reward for handling the Iola thing well—she was getting pretty good at lying, which was a bit worrying— but now, as she slid into the car, she knew the baggage thing was the least of her problems. For some reason all the rules about emotional engagement, rules which were essential for self-protection, had become fuzzy in the last twenty-four hours. This might be a rebound thing; she really didn't know any more but, whatever it was, it was powerful enough to cause her to cast aside every moral and principle she had lived by for the last twenty-eight years. *She wanted Blaine Morosini.*

Maisie tried to respond to Blaine's comment about it being a beautiful evening with a coherent reply even as her mind was in another galaxy.

She had never dreamt in a thousand years she could feel this way; in fact she had always had a slightly patronising pity for women who said they just couldn't resist a guy, but she was being forced to eat her words. Blaine had stirred feelings and emotions in her she'd never known existed and, although it was more scary than the worst cellulite, it was real.

She was still clutching the beautiful red rose and now she stroked its velvet petals as she said abstractedly, 'There are no thorns on this rose.'

'That's because it's not real.' At her look of surprise he added, 'Oh, I do not mean it is artificial; I was not talking in that sense. But this rose has been cultivated in protected surroundings and had all its sharp edges removed. It has never felt the rain on its petals or the insects landing on its leaves; it has not properly lived.'

'Poor rose.' She lifted it to her nose. 'And it only has the faintest perfume. Perhaps it's because it's had it too easy that it has no perfume? Perhaps it needed the rain and the wind and everything to bring out its true beauty, its fragrance?'

'Perhaps.' He glanced at her and he was smiling that slightly lopsided smile again, which was sheer dynamite because the rest of him was so utterly perfect. 'Or maybe we're not meant to be philosophers and are talking a load of rubbish?'

Maisie smiled back. She was unutterably relieved that he didn't appear to be offended or cross with her for her manipulation of tonight. Then again he might be fuming but hiding it under those Italian good manners and charm? She took a deep breath. She had to say something, now, at the beginning of the evening or she wouldn't be able to stand it. She had to make it clear she had asked him out for a good reason. 'Blaine, I know I shouldn't have put you in the position I did last night, about pretending you'd asked me out, I mean, but I had to talk to you and it looked as though you weren't planning to be around for a while.'

'No, I wasn't.'

'Oh.' For a second she was taken aback but then she rallied. It was going to be cards on the table and no dressing things up, was it? Fine. That suited her because if she didn't have her say over all this she would burst. 'The thing is, I'm someone who likes everything out in the open,' she said firmly. 'I know men have this tendency to keep stuff bottled up and think any emotional talk is just for women, but I don't like secrets or playing games. I'm not made like that.'

He shifted his legs and in the close confines of the car it registered on Maisie like a punch in the solar plexus.

She swallowed hard and went on, 'You said something about worrying that I was vulnerable last night when you...' She faltered.

'When I kissed you,' he put in softly.

'Yes. You said Jeff had taken away my self-esteem and that I was responding to you to prove something to myself, that I was still desirable. That's absolute rubbish.'

She saw him blink. He obviously wasn't used to quite such plain speaking from his women, she thought, but she had started now and she might as well say it all. She was going to be stark staring crazy if she didn't get this off her chest.

'I'm over Jeff,' she declared evenly. 'I don't know how it's happened so fast—' that was a lie but she was only going to go so far with this truth thing, and he probably knew it was because she had met him anyway '—but it has and I'm glad. We wouldn't have lasted. I think I was more a mother than a girlfriend to him.'

One black eyebrow rose quizzically. 'Whatever else, Maisie, rest assured I do not see you as a mother substitute.'

She knew that. From the way he had kissed her last night, she had no illusions on that score. 'So from my side there's no reason why you shouldn't—' hell, how did she say this? '—kiss me,' she finished weakly. 'Not from my side.'

'Meaning you suspect I have reasons why I do not wish to be in a relationship?'

Hearing it like that was a bit daunting, to say the least, especially when he had spoken in a tone of voice which suggested she was right. Maisie felt a fresh riot in her stomach, which came with the realisation that she might have done better to let sleeping dogs lie. She got the distinct impression she was forcing him to say things she didn't want to hear. 'I suppose so,' she managed after a long pause.

This time the pause went on even longer. 'Maisie,' said Blaine, just as she was ready to scream or burst into tears or both, 'I can't do togetherness. No, wrong, I do not want to do togetherness, but it's nothing to do with you. I want you. I might as well admit I've wanted you from the minute I set eyes on you when you rushed into that café all flushed and warm and ruffled—'

'Why?' She had to interrupt him because, being a man, he was making this ten times worse. 'Why can't you—why don't you *want* to be with someone? With *me*. Why don't you want to be with me?'

'It's a long story.'

'We've got time.'

'I don't talk about it.'

'Try,' she said through gritted teeth. Because if you don't, the way I'm feeling right now, I'll forget I'm a lady and do something I'll regret.

'I'm sorry, but it is pointless. Would you prefer me to turn the car round and take you home now?' It was final.

Maisie stared down at her toes. 'If you meant what you said, about even liking me a little bit, please tell me,' she whispered. 'I…I need to hear it.'

He swore very softly. She didn't know Italian but she did know a swear word when she heard it in any language. They drove on in silence for some moments and Maisie was quite oblivious to the clifftop views and scenic splendour. Eventually Blaine said, 'We will talk over dinner but not at the restaurant where I have reserved a table. I will cancel this. I will cook for you and we will talk, *sì*? With this you will be satisfied?'

She nodded. 'Yes.'

'But understand this, *mia piccola*. I have nothing to give you. Oh, I am a man, I have needs, but these can be sated without the heart being involved. There are many wealthy and influential career women who want commitment even less than I do; you understand what I am saying? They do not desire obligations and ties, they are content with a good time and their freedom. You are not like this, I see that. For you physical affection would mean more.'

Physical affection? He was talking about love-making without the love part. 'Surely that reduces us to animal level?' she said quietly. 'Not even that really, because animals often choose to be paired for life.'

He moved his head impatiently. 'It is possible for some men and women to enjoy each other's bodies with only friendship, rather than love, as the root emotion. Not everyone wants roses round the door, Maisie. Remember that. Just because you feel differently, it does not mean that they are wrong, merely that they have chosen an alternative way. The sexual act between a male and female is a very enjoyable one, regardless of whether they have rings on their fingers or not.'

It sounded well thought out and reasonable. And cold. Very cold. But Blaine wasn't a cold man, she knew that. What was really going on in his heart? And what sort of super woman had Francesca been to have the power to mess him up so completely? And—much, *much* more to the point—how could she, little Maisie Burns from England, even begin to compete? She couldn't. All she could do was be herself because she had nothing to lose, she saw that now. She'd lost him. Not that she had ever had him in the first place.

Maisie turned her head and looked out of the car window. 'I admit I don't see things the way you do,' she said quietly, 'and I believe absolutely in roses round the door. I believe some people are meant for each other and relationships like that are heaven on earth.'

'And the other kind can be hell on earth.'

'Look at your brother. He left Italy because he'd fallen for Jackie's mother and I know for sure they've been madly in love ever since. And then there's your own parents. They're happy, aren't they?'

'I do not deny this.' He sighed, raking his hair back from his brow and narrowing his eyes. 'But they are lucky. I am no longer prepared to take gambles. It is as simple as that. I run my life exactly how I want to and answer to no one.'

Well, bully for you. Frustration made her want to slap him. She wriggled in her seat. 'You might have an answer for everything but you're still wrong,' she said vehemently.

'I thought I might be,' murmured Blaine, his mouth curving.

How could he remain so calm and even *smile* when he was effectively slamming the door on any chance they had to be with each other? She shouldn't have come tonight. She should tell him he could do what he had suggested and turn the car round and take her back.

She glanced at him under her eyelashes. He looked hard and handsome and his very sexy mouth wasn't smiling any more. And there was no way, no way on earth, she was going to tell him to take her home.

CHAPTER EIGHT

MAISIE knew Positano was an exceptionally pretty Italian town with brightly coloured villas cascading down the cliffs to the sea, sleepy lanes and endless steep alleyways and wonderful cafés and beach restaurants serving freshly caught fish. She had asked Liliana all about the area where Blaine lived that afternoon. Apparently the centre of the town was pedestrianised and the very fashionable resort was popular with Italians, which would have meant almost for sure that Blaine would have had to talk to friends if they had gone to eat in any of the restaurants there. For that reason she was immensely glad they were having dinner at his home. If this was going to be the only evening she would ever share exclusively with him, she wanted to make the most of every minute.

As the Ferrari climbed up into the hills through lush vegetation Maisie could hear the chirping of crickets in the warm balmy air and, despite their unsettling conversation and the prospect of what she was going to hear later, she was fascinated by what she saw. The legendary coastline, the scent of the lemon and orange groves in the hillsides, the dappled evening sunshine and the sheer beauty all around her was breathtaking.

By unspoken mutual consent they had remained silent

since their earlier conversation, and it was Blaine who broke the silence to say quietly, 'My home welcomes you,' as he drove the car off the road and through open gates set in a shoulder-high whitewashed wall into a small paved area.

Maisie looked about her. Blaine's house was built at the top of and virtually into the cliffs. She imagined the view inside was wonderful. Ornate balconies bursting with brightly coloured pots of flowers faced her, and there was a curving staircase leading to the front door, which was a storey high from where they were standing.

'The house is on several levels,' Blaine said as they walked up the stairs. 'It is what you English would call quirky, I think.'

He had his suit jacket slung over one shoulder and his tie was hanging loose on either side of his shirt collar, the first few buttons undone. Maisie was overcome with such a rush of lust she almost missed her footing.

When they stepped into the house the first thing she noticed was how the sunlight lit up every corner. They were standing in a huge sprawling sitting room decorated and furnished in shades of coffee, biscuit and cream, the floor light wood and the main colour in the room coming from one long wall which was covered in decorative plates, glazed thickly like Arab pottery. A huge balcony looked over an awe-inspiring view of Positano, beyond which the azure waters of the ocean lay, and the balcony held a big table with six cushioned seats besides an array of lemon-scented verbenas, pink begonias, salvias and other flowers in terracotta pots which heavily perfumed the warm air.

'Oh, wow.' Maisie didn't even try to be blasé. 'This is the most incredible house.'

'You haven't seen it all yet,' Blaine said mildly, but she could tell he was pleased by her reaction.

All of it consisted of a beautifully fitted white oak and black marble kitchen and separate dining room on the floor below the sitting room. Through this a door led into a wide courtyard-style garden with tropical trees and shrubs and masses of tubs of flowers, an iron table and chairs again looking out over the wonderful view. The courtyard was built on the left side of the house and was totally private. The floor above the sitting room held two large bedrooms with a bathroom between them, both of which had balconies to take advantage of the view again, but it was the top floor which took Maisie's breath away. The master bedroom with its magnificent *en suite* bathroom in white and black marble was stunning. The wall which overlooked the ocean was made entirely of glass so that the occupants of the massive bed could see for miles and the balcony which stretched the length of the room also had panels of glass between its supports of stone so as not to impede the view from inside the room.

It wasn't only the view that was making Maisie breathless though. The huge bed with its black silk sheets and voluptuous pillows was unlike any bed Maisie had seen before and must have been built inside the room. It was a masterpiece of decadence. Along one wall was a full-length walk-in wardrobe and on the other were shelves set into the wall holding books, tapes, papers and various other objects Maisie's feverish gaze couldn't pick out. But it was when she glanced at the ceiling she nearly died. The area over the bed was captured by a huge circular mirror, blatant and unashamed and bold.

Blaine was standing by the door and had remained there while she looked around, his arms folded across his chest and his big body relaxed as he leant against the wood. When her gaze shot down from the ceiling and she coloured violently, she knew he had noticed. Had noticed and enjoyed her reaction. Forcing herself to look straight at him, Maisie said, 'This is very nice,' and even to her own ears her voice sounded prim.

'Nice? Is that the best you can do?' he reproved her gently. 'I spent a great deal of time planning this room.'

He was laughing at her. She knew he was laughing at her even though the dark handsome face betrayed no amusement. 'It's…unusual,' she said tightly. 'Very.'

'Very unusual.' He considered with his head slightly on one side. 'Thank you. I like to think so.'

'And…and very masculine. You know, being all black and white. Ascetic but luxurious at the same time. Was that the look you were trying to achieve?' she asked, her face hot.

'I don't think I was exactly interested in a look,' he murmured softly. 'I just wanted somewhere where I could relax and enjoy…the view.'

She knew what view he was talking about all right. The view of some gorgeous nude beauty in that mirror, a woman who would be more than happy to take what he could offer and not ask for more commitment than he wanted to give. Workaholic, her foot! He might not bring any women home to meet Mother but he sure didn't sit in this bed reading paperwork or dictating letters or whatever it was he did. Maisie didn't know if she felt angry or sad. She thought actually it was a mixture of both with a big dollop of jealousy and envy thrown in for good measure.

But she'd only got herself to blame for this, she admitted silently. He hadn't wanted to even see her tonight, let alone bring her to his house and certainly not his bedroom. Knowing that didn't help at all.

He was out of her league in every way, she told herself, pretending to look out of the glass doors leading to the balcony one last time. What on earth had she been doing in thinking there was a chance with him? Suddenly the loss of the few pounds in weight which had so cheered her earlier seemed utterly pathetic. Laughable. Not that she felt like laughing.

'Come downstairs and I'll fix you a drink while I change.' His voice was gentle, all amusement gone.

Maisie heard it with something like horror. Was he feeling sorry for her now? Pride brought her head up and injected a bright note into her voice. 'Lovely.' She turned from the view and sailed across the room, quite forgetting about the vertiginous sandals and almost doing the splits because of her mistake.

'Careful.' Blaine caught her in his arms as she catapulted forward, saving something of her dignity in the process but causing her a bigger problem when she found herself held against a hard male chest, his shirt smelling deliciously of some nice washing liquid.

'It's my sandals…' She glanced up at him when he didn't seem in any hurry to let her go. His eyes were piercing, their light trained on hers, and his face was very still. 'I…I'm not used to heels.'

'Your hair smells of apple blossom.' His voice was husky, preoccupied. 'And it's so silky and soft.' His fingertips were against her lower ribs, his palms cupping her sides, and the warmth of his flesh had robbed Maisie of the ability to speak. She simply continued to gaze up at him and then shut her eyes as he nuzzled his chin into her hair, drawing her closer.

When he put his mouth to hers it was a light stroking of her lips at first, his hands moving to trace the contours of her body through the thin dress. His mouth began an exploration of her cheeks, her nose, her eyes, his kisses burningly quick and sensuous. His breath was warm against her skin and her flesh tingled where the heat of his lips and hands touched, her legs becoming fluid as she turned her face to capture his mouth again.

Like before, a multitude of new feelings were coursing through her and she was enchanted and bewitched by the power of his caresses, her body fitting into his like a natural jigsaw when he urged her even harder against the hard length of him. A slowly growing ache was seeping through every cell of her body as she gave herself up to the magic he was creating, coherent thought long since gone, her eyes closing again.

'Maisie, Maisie.' He breathed her name, his voice throaty and shaky, each kiss and caress hungrier and more intimate.

Somehow she found herself on the huge billowing bed, although she hadn't been aware of being led there. The rich black silk smelt ever so faintly of his aftershave and it touched her skin like warm cream as she opened her eyes in bemused surprise. 'Blaine?' she said dazedly.

He had been about to peel the bodice of the dress away from the swollen fullness of her breasts, their engorged tips hard from the contact of his body. Now he froze, his heavily lashed glittering eyes opening wider. 'Hell,' he said.

He was breathing hard, his chest rising and falling under the thin shirt as he fought for control for long seconds. Then he slowly rose, walking across to the glass doors, which led on to the balcony and keeping his back to her as he said roughly, 'You see? You see how it is with you? I cannot keep my hands off you.'

But she didn't *want* him to, so what was the problem? Maisie sat up, trembling from head to toe and fumbling with her dress, which was round her thighs, as she said, 'Why does that matter?'

She watched as he shook his head and now his voice was

colder. 'It matters because you are not the sort of woman a man takes to bed for one night and then forgets about, neither would you be content to be a number in a little black book. You are Jackie's friend, for crying out loud, a *family* friend; you are living with my parents, working for them.' He stopped abruptly, straightening his shoulders, but still not turning to look at her as he added, 'It was madness to bring you here tonight.'

The thrill that he wanted her, that he was actually finding it hard to keep his hands off her, was completely negated by the way he was talking. However attracted he was to her, his autonomy mattered more. That was what he was saying. Maisie slid off the bed, smoothing down her dress and running her fingers through her tousled hair to tidy it. She wanted to burst into tears but she knew that would just make a bad situation a hundred times worse. She had to salvage something out of this awful mess, a mess she had brought about by forcing his hand. They were going to come into contact with each other over the next weeks while she was staying at his parents' house; she didn't want him to stay away once his father was home because of her or anything like that.

She took a deep breath. 'OK,' she said steadily. 'I see where you're coming from. We'll put this down to experience, shall we, but I don't see any reason why we can't be friends. Just friends. And if you're ready, I'd like that drink now.' She would like a whole bottle actually; she'd need that much to get through the rest of the evening.

He turned, surveying her with a narrowed stare. She could see the intelligent mind whirring away, computing what she had just said. She waited, looking back at him without giving anything away.

'You think that is possible?' he said grimly. 'After what we have just shared? With all that is between us?'

It had to be. If she had thought some of the things she had gone through in the past were difficult, they were nothing compared to what she was having to do now. She forced herself to shrug nonchalantly. 'A few kisses, a little lovemaking,' she said evenly. 'That's all we shared and we are both mature adults after all.' Pride was coming to the rescue now— a little belatedly, admittedly, she thought bitterly, but better late than never. She was not going to grovel or beg for what he refused to give. Never in a million years. 'Perhaps we needed to do that to get it out of our system. Anyway, we've tried it and that's that. Friendship from now on. Agreed?'

He rubbed his hand across his mouth, clearly at a loss.

'And, like I said, I'm ready for that drink now. And dinner. Preferably before midnight.' She smiled and he would never know how much it cost. She turned from him, from the look in his eyes, and left the room, walking carefully down the winding staircase right down to the dining room and then out of the door into the fragrant courtyard. She sat down at the table, staring at the crystalline blue water in the distance and deliberately emptying her mind of all thought.

A few moments later he joined her, two glasses of deep red wine in his hands. She looked up, holding out her hand for a glass as she said, 'Thanks. What are we having for dinner?'

He grimaced. 'It will not be as exciting as if I had had time to plan for the occasion, but I thought perhaps ginger and chilli tiger prawns followed by tortelloni filled with ricotta and parsley, served with fresh lobster?'

'Wow.' She tried not to notice how the blue of the sky was reflected in his eyes. It wouldn't help. If he could do this, so could she. 'The mind boggles at what you would do if you *did* have time to plan.' She took a sip of the wine. It was smooth and soft, bursting with blackcurrant, cherry and violet aromas. 'Do you want me to do anything in the kitchen while you shower and change?' she asked, matching her voice to a tone she'd use if she was asking Jackie the same question.

He had swallowed half of his glass of wine. Now he set it down on the table. 'The only thing I want you to do is to refill your glass when you're ready,' he said, walking back into the dining room as he spoke and then exiting again with the bottle in his hand.

'Suits me.' She kicked off her sandals and wriggled her toes. If they were going to do this friendship thing then she might as well be comfortable. The extra couple of inches the sandals had given her didn't matter now, nor the way they'd made her ankles look tiny. She was done with trying to seduce him. And she was utterly, *utterly* fed up with men in general. The urge to cry was there again and she hoped he was going to clear off for his shower before she spoilt everything she'd achieved in the last few minutes.

Once he had disappeared, however, a feeling of reckless-ness took over and, draining her glass, she poured herself another. The evening had mellowed to one of satisfying warmth after the heat of the day, a thousand summers in the light breeze perfumed with sun-warmed vegetation and flowers. She didn't want to think any more, she found. She just wanted to be. Thinking was too painful, too unsettling.

When Blaine joined her a little while later she absolutely refused to dwell on the fact that he looked doubly sexy with his hair still damp from the shower. He had shaved and there was the tiniest of nicks on his chin. Why that should make her quiver inside she didn't know, but it did. Right down to her toes.

He had brought another bottle of the heavenly wine out with him and after refilling his own glass he raised his eyebrows as she put a hand over her own half full one. 'No more yet,' she said smilingly, telling herself she had to pretend he was Sue or Jackie or another of her friends and be as relaxed as she would be with them. 'I feel a bit tiddly, to tell you the truth.'

'After one and a half glasses?' He grinned back at her and she felt a rush of pure resentment that he could do this friendly thing so much easier than she could. 'Something tells me you are not a seasoned drinker.'

Unlike some of these sophisticated career women he had spoken about, no doubt. She supposed they could down a bottle without blinking. They could probably do a lot of things without blinking. Frequently. With him. 'I don't drink much,' she said airily, 'if that's what you mean.' On her salary she hadn't been able to afford to. And quite often when she and Jeff had gone out to dinner or eaten a meal at his very nice flat in central London, he'd been on call, so they'd shared nothing more exciting than a bottle of fizzy water. She briefly wondered how the perfect Camellia would react to his disappearing at the drop of a hat in the middle of a date. Badly, she hoped. She was completely over him but that didn't mean she wouldn't like him to get a bit of grief.

'The prawns will take about ten minutes so I'll get cooking.'

'Can I come and watch?' This sitting in splendid isolation was all very well and the view was undoubtedly stupendous, but compared to observing Blaine under the guise of watching him cook it couldn't even begin to compare. Sad. Maisie mentally nodded. She was turning into one sad female.

'Of course.' he nodded to her glass. 'Bring your wine.'

Once in the kitchen, she had to admit she was more than a little impressed by how organised and efficient he was. When she cooked anything other than a casserole, where she could sling everything in together and bung it in the oven, it tended to be something of a hit and miss affair, and she knew she was a messy cook. Blaine, on the other hand, was definitely a pro. She said as much once he had finished browning the sesame seeds and put them to one side, using the same pan with new oil to start cooking the prawns, garlic, chilli and green pepper.

'I am Italian,' he said matter-of-factly. 'It is in the genes, you know? Whenever Liliana visits her sister in Tuscany my father always cooks at home. My mother is not particularly domesticated.'

There you see, they would be absolutely perfect together. He could cook and she could watch him every night. Bliss. Maisie silently warned herself to stop. He didn't want her. Well, he did want her but not enough. End of story.

After Blaine had added the ginger cordial and sesame seeds to the pan and cooked for a further minute or so, he divided the contents between two plates on which nestled a green salad. They carried their plates and wine out to the courtyard and ate under the blue Italian sky. Maisie thought she had never understood how something could be bitter-sweet until tonight.

She didn't accompany him back to the kitchen for the second course but sat sipping her wine as she watched the sun go down. The shadow-blotched courtyard was still as warm as toast, even when the sky became streaked with tumescent crimson and enriched with bands of gold.

A violet dusk was settling when Blaine brought out the plates, and the tortelloni and lobster was every bit as delicious as the first course had been. He set out to be amusing and entertaining while they ate, the perfect host, and in spite of how Maisie was feeling inside she found herself giggling and enjoying herself. Probably the three glasses of red wine she had consumed by the time her plate was empty helped.

'And now for dessert.' Blaine's teeth were very white as he smiled at her in the indigo shadows. 'I cannot take the credit for these. There is an excellent little patisserie in Positano. You can choose from Sicilian lemon tart or pistachio cake.'

Maisie groaned. 'I can't eat another thing. I thought I'd lost some weight before I came here tonight but I'm sure I've put it all on again. I shall go back to England looking like the Michelin woman.'

'I do not think so,' he said softly. 'Just beautiful.'

That was the wrong tone of voice for friends, besides which it wasn't fair to say she was beautiful. Friends wouldn't say that. Jackie or Sue would have agreed with her and put in their own suggestions, like one of the Roly-Polys or a jelly on a plate. Maisie frowned, her sense of being misused aided and abetted by the fact that he hadn't the grace to even pretend to look devastated at the thought of her going back to England. 'No dessert for me, thank you,' she said firmly. 'Really. Just coffee.'

Blaine ate a gargantuan piece of lemon tart along with his coffee and although Maisie's mouth was watering she restrained herself from saying she'd changed her mind. The moon was out now, shedding a thin hollow light over the face of the ocean far below. The night was very still; even the light breeze of an hour or so ago had died away, leaving a sense of enduring timelessness in its place. They sipped their coffee without talking and then Blaine said quietly, 'We have eaten and now it is time, sì?'

Maisie glanced at him quickly. She knew he was talking about the explanation she had asked for. She also knew he was reluctant to give it. The evidence was there in the sudden tautness to the handsome features and the stiff line of his body. 'It's not necessary,' she said, equally quietly. Not now. 'I thought it was, but it really isn't.'

It was almost as though he hadn't heard her. 'Her name was Francesca,' he said flatly. 'She was my wife. We married when I graduated from university and took my place in the family business. We had been promised to each other from childhood.' He shrugged. 'It is the way things are done sometimes and I had no complaints. I had grown up loving her.'

Maisie was as still as a mouse. His *wife*? Stupid, but she had never expected that he had been married, somehow.

'She was twenty-two years old when we married. Within the year she was expecting our child and this triggered the mental condition which ran in her family. Of course this was not mentioned before the wedding.' He smiled grimly. 'My parents later admitted they had wondered why Francesca's parents had left Florence and settled in Sorrento, and why they never visited their respective families or had them to stay. It was the stigma, you see. Her father's mother had had the condition and her mother before her. It was suggested that because her father was a boy this condition had not affected him.' He shrugged. 'I do not know if this was so, only that Francesca became a different person almost overnight.'

'Blaine, you don't have to go on.' Maisie felt awful. If she had known, if she had even suspected just the slightest she wouldn't have pressed him for an explanation.

'At first I didn't know what I was dealing with,' he said painfully. 'I thought it was a kind of normal depression, if there is such a thing. I imagined with help she would snap out of it. Then her parents told her the truth. They had always said that all their family was dead and Francesca had grown up believing this. When they told her she became convinced there was no hope for her.'

He raked back his hair, moving restlessly in his chair before going on. 'My parents and I brought in the best doctors; they were optimistic that once the child was born and she could receive certain medication she would be a different woman. Not cured exactly, but if she stayed on the medication she would cope.'

He sat forward in his chair, his arms resting on his knees and his hands clasped in front of him. Somewhere close by a dog barked and then all was still again.

'She lost the baby at four months. Perhaps it was for the best, I don't know. We began the medication. Sometimes for long periods she was fine. Other times...she wasn't.'

The pause said much more than words could have done. Maisie could not see his face clearly in the shadowed darkness but she didn't have to. She knew it would be etched with pain. She sat stiff and still, scarcely breathing.

'And gradually over a period of time my feelings began to change. Oh, she did not know this—at least I think she did not know—but even in the early days of our marriage, before she became ill, I knew I had made a mistake. Francesca...she did not like the physical side of marriage. She would do her duty as she saw it but that was all. Maybe I should have recognised the signs before we married; she was always happy to cuddle and kiss a little but anything else and I was gently rebuffed. But she was a good Italian girl and I had been brought up to respect this. I did not expect more. After she lost the baby we lived virtually as brother and sister.'

How could any woman not want Blaine to make love to her? Maisie stared at his profile, wondering what that must have done to him.

'To all intents and purposes ours seemed a loving marriage to the outside world. Even, perhaps, to Francesca. She had the kudos of being married, which was important to her, having been raised by parents who believed in the old way. She had a nice home close to her parents—we lived in Sorrento—and she had me to take her out and look after her. She wanted nothing more, she made that very clear. Even in her good times any advances I made were not well received. And so life went on. Maybe if she had not been ill, things would have been different. I might have insisted she try to change. As it was, I realised I had made my bed and I had to lie on it. Alone, of course.' He smiled bitterly.

'You…couldn't have asked for a divorce?' Maisie said tentatively.

'Francesca was a staunch Catholic, like her parents, besides which I could not abandon her and cast her aside. It would have finished her. Again, if she had not been ill it would have been different.'

'She was lucky to have you.'

He looked up and into her eyes. 'Do not think of me as a saint, Maisie,' he said quietly. 'I am not proud of it, but by the time she became ill with leukaemia I think I almost hated her. She used her illness as a weapon and we both knew it. I resented her more than words can say; I longed for my freedom. Not in the way it happened—never that—but I wanted to be rid of her. My only comfort is that she did not know. I acted the part of the loving husband to the end.'

She stared at him, chilled in spite of the warm air. 'Was the leukaemia connected with her other illness?'

'No, just a fluke. But with hindsight I think it saved my sanity. I had lived a lie for almost a decade and it had taken a toll I was not aware of. I stood at her graveside and looked round at the weeping women and sombre-faced men and wondered what they would think if they knew how I was really feeling.'

'How did you feel?' she whispered.

'Like a bird released from a cage must feel.' He shook his head. 'As I said, I am not proud of it but it is the truth. I have not spoken of this before,' he added, his eyes moving to the ocean.

'Not to anyone?'

'When Francesca was alive it would have seemed like a betrayal. Afterwards…' He shrugged. 'It was no longer important.'

No longer important? It had changed him radically by his own admission, shaped him into the man he was now. A man who wanted complete and absolute autonomy, who would fight against any emotional commitment or ties single-mindedly. Of course it was important. She sucked in a breath, wondering how she could say what she was thinking. In the end, she murmured, 'I think it was a mistake not to at least share the truth with your parents. They could have helped you. And what about the future? What about a family one day, children? Don't you want that?'

'Once, but not now.' He turned to look at her again, his eyes glittering in the shadows. 'I never again want to be responsible for another human being.'

It was unequivocal. Maisie experienced a sensation akin to an elephant sitting on her heart and squeezing all the life out of it. She nodded in what she hoped was an understanding way. 'I can appreciate that, with what you've been through.'

'That's why I keep my relationships pretty simple these days.'

Hmm. Well, that was one way to put it.

'Of course Liliana would love to see me arrive with someone on my arm one day but it's not going to happen.'

OK, she had actually already got the message. 'So your life is a series of one-night stands?' she asked bluntly.

He blinked. 'Not exactly.'

Exactly what would he call it then? Maisie raised enquiring eyebrows. 'No?'

'I've told you, I date women who feel the same way as me.'

'But only for one night.'

'I'm not some kind of male stud, Maisie.' He was frowning now but she found she didn't care. 'They're mostly business colleagues, and of that nature, and as it happens I haven't been out with a woman for some months. I saw the last one a few times and then she moved to Sardinia with her job.'

'And that was too far for you to go and see her?'

'Neither of us wanted that.' His tone was becoming steely but considering he had laid it on the line for her she felt she had nothing to lose.

She nodded. 'So you see the rest of your life in terms of being independent and self-sufficient and alone basically?'

He deliberately poured himself another cup of coffee from the pot on the table and drank some of it before he said, 'Is there a point you are trying to make?'

Damn right. It was a terrible waste, for one thing. 'Just that you are going to end up a very lonely old man when you don't have to,' she said bravely, ignoring his expression. 'I can see your marriage must have been a nightmare for much of the time, but that doesn't mean you couldn't be happy with someone else.' Like me, for instance. Fat chance.

'I don't see it that way.'

No, well she supposed he didn't, and who was she to try and persuade him otherwise anyway? Maybe one of these gorgeous, bright, well-sorted career women he mixed with might have a chance, but her? You'd have to be pretty special to bag a man like Blaine in the first place and hanging on to him would be even harder, even without all his hang-ups.

Maisie finished the last of her now cold coffee. 'I'm sorry

it all went so wrong for you, Blaine,' she said softly as she put the cup down. 'I hope you'll find happiness again one day.' And she meant it, she did—as long as she wasn't around to see him with someone else.

'Thank you.' His voice was equally low. 'So we are still friends, *sì*?'

Maisie nodded.

'And as friends maybe I could show you a little of my country over the next weeks once my mother is home? She will still need some help with the animals, of course, but there will be things she will prefer to do. I know this.' His voice was wry. 'She cannot, how do you say, sit around and twiddle her fingers all day.'

'Her thumbs.'

'*Sì*, her thumbs.'

It was rare that his excellent English let him down and Maisie felt a rush of something she would rather not put a name to flood her being. Dangerous, dangerous man—she had told herself this before and she ignored it at her peril. She nodded mentally to the warning.

'So, we do some sightseeing, Maisie?'

'If you're sure you have the time.' She was forewarned, wasn't she? she told the little voice in her head which was screaming that she was mad. And forewarned is forearmed. That was what they said. She just hoped they—whoever they were—were right.

CHAPTER NINE

GUISEPPE came home a few days later and as soon as Maisie saw Blaine's father she knew she was going to like him. He looked like an older version of Roberto, being plump, a little on the short side and with twinkly eyes. Blaine didn't resemble him in the least.

Guiseppe was too exhausted by the journey to talk much that first evening, but the next day Maisie kept him company and got to know him while Jenny spent rapturous quality time with the foal and the proud parents. Maisie had phoned a friend who had married a Welshman and was living in Wales for help in choosing an appropriate name for the little animal. It had to be Welsh, to begin with and mean something nice, she'd told them—and the name Ithel, meaning generous lord had been drawn from the pot. Jenny had pronounced herself delighted with the name so Ithel it was.

It was in the late afternoon, when Maisie and Guiseppe were sitting on the veranda drinking some of Liliana's delicious homemade lemonade and watching Jenny cavort in the paddock with the horses, that Guiseppe told her that things were all right between Roberto and himself now.

'I'm glad.' Maisie smiled into the tired eyes. 'And I know his family will be.'

'I have been a foolish man, Maisie. Oh, yes, I have,' he added as though she had been about to protest. She hadn't. She agreed with him. 'But Roberto has promised to bring his wife and children and grandchildren out to Italy at the end of the summer. It seems strange to realise I have grandchildren and even great-grandchildren I knew nothing about.'

So much wasted time. Maisie didn't say what she was thinking because there was no point in rubbing salt in the wound, but Guiseppe must have guessed anyway because he said, 'There are always consequences to our foolishness, are there not? I have missed what could have been a wonderful time because of my stubbornness. I thank God for Jenny, do you know that? She had been saying for years I should make my peace with my son, but I was too proud to make the first move. Crazy, eh?'

'Very.' She smiled to soften the word. 'And I think your son was just as bad.'

'*Sì, sì.*' He shook his head sorrowfully. 'My elder son takes after me rather than his mother, this is true. His mother was a sweet gentle soul; she would have despaired of the pair of us, I think. Now Blaine is very much a mixture of Jenny and myself and this is good.'

Maisie didn't know about that. She thought there was far more of Guiseppe than Jenny in Blaine. Again her face must have given her away because Guiseppe's eyes were suddenly keen on hers as he said, 'What is it? Blaine has upset you in some way?'

'Not at all.' Maisie forced a bright smile. 'I'm going to Capri with him the day after tomorrow, as it happens. He wants to show me a little of Italy before I have to go back home.'

Guiseppe continued to examine her for some moments. Then he said, 'I see.'

She doubted that very much but she could hardly say, But we're only friends, or else that would look as though she was thinking Guiseppe suspected something else. Which she did think, of course, but she couldn't let him know that. Instead she said, a little lamely, 'I split up with my fiancé just before I came out here, you see. I think Blaine feels a bit sorry for me.'

Guiseppe looked at the smooth-skinned pretty girl in front of him, her silky hair caught in a high ponytail, which made her look little more than a teenager and her large brown eyes velvet dark and shadowed by thick lashes. His voice was dry when he murmured, 'Blaine is not in the habit of feeling sorry for people.'

Maisie knew her cheeks were burning, but other than blurting out everything that had passed between her and Blaine—which was *so* not an option—she knew she couldn't say anything to convince him he was on the wrong tack. 'I'd better see about feeding the dogs and cats,' she said, standing up and so dislodging Humphrey, who was sitting on her foot as usual. And she would make sure she took the dogs for a long walk later, about the time Blaine would call in on his way home. He had told Jenny he'd do that the night before and at the time her heart had leapt at the thought of being able to see him for a while. Now she knew it wasn't a good idea, not till he'd put his father straight about them being just good friends anyway. And if she was out of the way she was fairly sure Guiseppe would mention it.

She didn't breathe easy until she had escaped from the house just before Blaine was due. The dogs were quite ecstatic when they all set off, but by the time she had walked their paws off in an effort to make sure Blaine would be gone when she got back, they weren't so frisky. She had told Jenny and Guiseppe she didn't want any dinner; she had a headache, she'd lied, and wanted a long walk in the fresh air to clear it, so it was getting dark when she returned to the villa and she was absolutely ravenous.

She was going to be as thin as a rake at this rate, she comforted herself later in the privacy of her room, demolishing the two apples and banana in the fruit bowl on her dressing table in two minutes flat. She had eaten the orange and other banana before she left the house. It was scant reward for missing seeing Blaine. She sighed heavily to herself as the telephone rang and someone in the house picked it up.

A moment or two later there was a discreet tap at her door. When she opened it, Liliana said, 'The telephone, Maisie. It is for you, *sì*?' She gestured to the extension next to the empty fruit bowl.

'Me?' Must be Jackie. 'Thanks, Liliana.'

'Your headache? It is better after the pills?'

Guiseppe and Jenny had retired when she'd returned to the villa ten minutes or so ago, but Liliana had still been busy in the kitchen. To avoid having to talk, Maisie had kept to her story of the headache and had taken the two painkillers Liliana had insisted she swallow before coming up to bed. 'Much, thanks.'

Shutting the door again, Maisie then picked up the phone. 'Hallo?' she said, quite expecting Jackie to answer.

'Hallo, Maisie.' The deep smoky voice definitely wasn't female. 'How's the headache?'

She found she was regretting the headache story more every time someone asked her how it was. 'Much better, thank you,' she lied again, ignoring the bolt of electricity that had shot through her at the sound of Blaine's voice.

'Good.' There was a pause and then he said, 'I didn't know if you were avoiding me.'

'Avoiding you?' She gave a trill of a laugh she was quite

proud of in the circumstances. 'Why ever would I be avoiding you, Blaine?'

The pause was even longer this time. 'I wasn't sure if you were…comfortable about coming to Capri with me.'

About as comfortable as being stretched over a bed of nails. 'Of course, why wouldn't I be?' she said brightly.

He didn't answer this. Instead he said softly, 'It wasn't the same without you at the house. Too quiet.'

Oh, no, she wasn't doing this. She had virtually thrown herself at him the other night and he had made it abundantly clear there could never be anything between them. Apart from friendship. And even the friendship thing had come from her, if she came to think about it. 'It was only quiet because the dogs were out,' she said. 'Nothing to do with me.'

'Right. I never thought of that.'

Maisie frowned into the phone. He might at least have had the grace to argue the point. 'Why are you calling, Blaine?'

'If you were a girlfriend—rather than a friend without the girl before it—I'd say it was to hear the sound of your voice.'

'But I'm not and you aren't, so why did you call?'

'Are you in a bad mood?' he asked silkily.

'Not in the least.' Irritating, impossible man.

'So this is you in a good mood with nothing at all wrong then?'

'You know what's wrong. I've got a—'

'Headache,' he finished for her. 'But I thought it was better?'

'I said it was much better, not that it had gone. And how much better it is depends on how bad it was in the first place. And it was bad. Terrible.'

'Then I had better leave you to sleep. You must be tired after your hike in the hills, *sì*?' he said smoothly.

She had been feeling quite tired but now there was enough

adrenaline surging about her body to keep her awake until dawn. 'Liliana gave me two painkillers,' she said, glad that at least that was the truth. 'They do make one drowsy.' That wasn't.

'Sweet dreams, *mia piccola*.' It was gentle, almost tender.

'Goodnight, Blaine.' Maisie found her hand was shaking when she put down the receiver. So what had all that been about? She sat down on her bed with a plump and after re-running their conversation in her mind several times found she was no nearer as to why Blaine had called. She had asked him but he hadn't answered; in fact he had sidestepped the question very neatly.

It was when she found herself pacing the room that commonsense kicked in. What was she doing? What on earth was she doing? Very probably Blaine's father had said something about him taking her out for the day, as she had thought he might, and it had set Blaine wondering if she was OK about this platonic matey thing. He had been ringing to see if she wanted to back out of seeing him, that was it. Probably he'd been rather hoping she might. And as for that note in his voice when he had said goodbye, that was her fooling herself. If you were desperate enough you could make yourself believe anything.

Not that she was desperate, not really. She liked him, of course, she liked him very much and certainly the attraction thing had opened her eyes to a side of life she'd previously only read about in books, but that boiled down to lust, plain and simple. Only it wasn't plain; it was very, very complicated and confusing, and it certainly wasn't simple.

She stood scowling with her hands on her hips for a full minute before walking into the bathroom and running herself a warm bath. This time she stayed in the water until it was almost cold, graphic pictures of Blaine naked in that wicked bed—or in the shower, or even cooking with just a small apron to protect certain vital parts from splashes—running through her mind and ensuring she left the water as tense and upright as when she'd slid under the warm bubbles.

She would have to stay around tomorrow night when he called in to see his father, especially as they were going to Capri the next day. After drying her hair and pulling on a thin nightie, Maisie slid under the cool cotton covers and tried to relax. And she had to stop getting herself into such a state over this man. It was ridiculous; she had another few weeks in Italy yet, and she couldn't carry on like this. The ground rules had been set, the situation was clear, everything was straightforward. It was only her silly feelings that were muddying the water. Well, all that stopped right now. She began the breathing exercises she had learnt during a yoga phase some years previously and, to her surprise, they worked. Within five minutes she was fast asleep.

She supposed she should have expected that Blaine's mother might ask him to stay for dinner the next evening and that he might accept, but nevertheless she felt a moment of acute panic when it happened. As it was, it turned out to be a very pleasant meal in a convivial atmosphere, due mainly to Guiseppe's ongoing improvement, with no awkward silences or long pauses.

Maisie was more convinced than ever that Blaine had set his parents straight about there being no romantic involvement possible between them as the evening progressed. Which was fine, just fine, she told herself firmly. It removed the likelihood of any misconception for a start. Now, when Jenny praised her for how well she cared for the animals and how even the cats had been persuaded to succumb to their grooming without their normal spitting and cuffs, Maisie knew it was because Blaine's mother really meant it. And when Guiseppe commented over the dessert that her presence in the house had made him think they had missed out by not having a daughter, she knew he wasn't just trying to be nice for Blaine's sake.

On her part, she found herself liking Jenny and Guiseppe more every hour of every day. Never having got on with her own mother, she found Jenny's easy warm nature a delight, and Guiseppe, although undeniably fiery and somewhat difficult, was essentially a kind man with a loving heart.

All through the meal, however, even as she chatted and laughed and joined in the flowing conversation, she was vitally aware of the tall dark man on the other side of the table. Blaine was one of those men whose every action, every look or expression was just totally masculine. He exuded maleness—virile, flagrant maleness—and it made her toes curl.

She had prepared herself once she sat down at the table, though, and when their glances happened to meet or if they talked to each other she kept a tight rein on her surging hormones. She was not going to make a fool of herself over him again, she had promised herself that.

Once the meal was over it was obvious Guiseppe was very tired. The major heart surgery he had undertaken had been an enormous shock to his body, and when Jenny insisted on saying goodnight to Blaine and Maisie and ushering Guiseppe to their quarters he didn't object too much. Blaine and Maisie sat finishing their coffee in the ornate grandeur of the dining room, and for the first time that evening Maisie found herself tongue-tied. Probably because she had caught herself fantasising about what it would be like for a woman to lose her virginity to a strong sexy man like Blaine Morosini. Bad idea. Not the losing of it, of course, but the thinking about it.

'I'm looking forward to tomorrow,' Blaine murmured after several tense moments.

Tense on her side, Maisie noted irritably. Blaine didn't seem bothered at all.

'It has been a long time since I showed off the beauty of my country to a visitor,' he added lazily.

Which was the only reason he was looking forward to a day spent in her company? Charming. Maisie's edginess melted into impotent anger. She smiled sweetly. 'Me, too,' she said very calmly. 'It's always so much better to see the sights with a friend who knows the area.' She reached for one of the glaringly calorific homemade chocolates Liliana had brought in with the coffee earlier. She needed the comfort factor.

'We will spend another day in Amalfi, I think.' Blaine smiled at her and her traitorous nerves buzzed. 'Do you know how the town got its name?'

Maisie shook her head. She didn't much care either, but if it kept him here with her an extra few minutes she'd even listen to talk about football or cricket.

'According to tradition, Hercules fell in love with a beautiful nymph called Amalfi,' Blaine said softly, 'but they only had a short time together before she sadly died. Hercules decided to bury his love in what he considered to be the most beautiful place on earth, and to immortalise her he gave it her name.'

'That's very sad.'

'Most legends are.' Blaine grinned at her. 'But Amalfi is worth a visit. We will go on a Friday evening, I think. In the cathedral there the atrium leads to the lovely Chiostro del Paradiso, the Paradise Cloister, an Arabian structure built in the thirteenth century and the setting for piano concerts in the summer months on a Friday evening. You will enjoy this.'

Maisie stared at him. How often had he gone there with Francesca? Or other women?

'Then there are the exquisite ancient mosaics and Roman treasures in the museum in Naples, the ruins of Pompeii, the cathedral at Ravello where the blood of St Pantaleone miraculously liquefies twice a year…' He paused. 'And so I could go on. You will fall in love with Italy. I guarantee it.'

She had fallen in love. And not just with Italy. As the thought struck her stomach clenched and she bent to pick up her napkin, which had fallen on the floor, to hide her expression from him. *She loved him.* It had been staring her in the face for days but she hadn't wanted to believe it. This wasn't an emotional rebound thing or a holiday infatuation, it was real. It made the way she had felt about Jeff, Gary too, so lukewarm as to be laughable.

She sat up again, placing the napkin on the table and smoothing her hair from her face as she said, 'Blaine, I'm supposed to be working for your mother. I can't just go gallivanting off every day.' Not that she didn't want to be with him, but every minute she was there was the very real danger she would betray herself. And that humiliation would be too much to bear on top of everything else.

'My mother adores you; it is not a problem. Besides which, it will not be every day,' he said in a reasonable tone which suggested she was grossly exaggerating. 'Now—' he stood up and Maisie wondered why it was some men could move with the grace of one of the big cats '—I will be here for you at seven o'clock in the morning, *sì*?'

She nodded, following him out into the hall and then to the front door. He opened it before turning round and skimming her cheeks with his warm mouth. The Latin caress was the same as he had given his parents before they had retired for the night and she knew it meant nothing; nevertheless it set every nerve clamouring. It took every ounce of will she possessed to betray nothing but neutrality when she said, 'Goodnight, Blaine.'

'Goodnight, *mia piccola*. Sleep well.'

She stood watching him as he walked to his car and she was glad of the shadows as her eyes suddenly pricked with tears. Why couldn't it have been different? Why couldn't she have been so beautiful, so desirable, that all his fears about getting involved faded into nothing? Why did she have to be Maisie Burns?

She stood on the doorstep in the quiet warmth of the scented evening long after Blaine's car had disappeared. And then she sighed heavily, shut the door and walked upstairs, telling herself she must, she *must*, get her crazy feelings under control and just take each day as it came and be thankful for it. To live for the minute, the hour, without thinking beyond that.

In a few weeks she would be returning to England, just in time for the autumn chill to begin and for winter to start making its presence felt with the usual icy rain and fogs and damp mornings. All this would seem like a dream then. Blaine Morosini would seem like a dream.

Once in her bedroom she didn't immediately start undressing but stood at the window, gazing out at the black sky twinkling with a thousand stars.

He had made it crystal clear how he felt. She could expect nothing. And if she was foolish enough to hope for more it would be her own fault when she was disappointed. And if, being a man and an Italian one at that, he flirted a little during the coming days when he took her out she had to accept it as a compliment to her femininity and nothing more.

She was glad now that he had stopped making love to her that night he had taken her to his home. Glad that he had been brutally honest with her, however painful it had been at the time. If they had had a short-lived affair, if he had been the sort of man who had strung her along with the well-used glib line about 'seeing how things went', she wouldn't have been able to stand it when he had walked away from her. She was an all or nothing woman. She had never seen it so clearly in all her life. And as it couldn't be all, it had to be nothing.

CHAPTER TEN

MAISIE found her thoughts of the previous night put to the test the next day. The morning was promising to be hot when Blaine arrived at seven o'clock, and the drive down to Sorrento's harbour where they were boarding the boat for Capri was under a sky as blue as cornflowers. Not that Maisie noticed the colour of the sky; it could have been bright pink and covered in polka dots and she still wouldn't have noticed. She was having too much trouble adjusting to the sight of Blaine in an open-necked black denim shirt, his black jeans, tight across the hips, designer cut and revealing the awesome length of his legs. She had never seen him dressed so casually before; normally he was in his workday suits or expertly cut trousers and crisp shirts and he looked good enough in those. Today, though, the magnetism that was at the heart of his flagrant masculinity was emphasised ten-fold.

By the time they reached the golden island on the Gulf of Naples Maisie had herself under control, though. It helped that Blaine seemed totally unaware of his ability to turn her legs to jelly. In fact overnight he had metamorphosised into the perfect 'just friends' companion, eager to show her all there was to be seen, amusing, communicative and thoughtful.

Immediately they stepped off the boat Maisie could understand why Augustus had described Capri as the 'city of sweet idleness', its cliffs that descended rapidly into the sea and gardens bedecked with subtropical vegetation amazing. Already captivated by the bewitching island, everything was made so much better by Blaine's lazy insistence of holding her hand as he showed her the sights.

They visited the luminous caverns of the Blue Grotto, the Gardens of Augustus, with stunning views stretching to the jutting needles of the Faraglioni and Pizzolungo rocks, and later the equally stunning views from the summit of Monte Solaro. They ate exquisitely prepared seafood risotto and insalata Caprese, made with mozzarella and home-grown tomatoes, at a harbourside restaurant at Marina Grande, before thoroughly exploring the maze of alleyways and squares of the main town. They had coffee and pastries at the popular La Piazzetta during the afternoon and sat for a while watching the world go by, before more exploring.

It was a wonderful magical day, the beginning of several as Blaine held true to his promise to show her more of his beloved Italy over the next weeks. Maisie found it was impossible not to look forward with a physical ache to these golden sojourns out of reality, and that was what they were, she kept reminding herself once she was back at his parents' villa and alone again. Blaine himself had emphasised this, not so much by what he said and did but by what he didn't do and say.

He held her hand but there were no passionate embraces. He kissed her, as a friend would kiss a friend, on the cheek and never on the mouth. His arm would slip round her waist on occasion, but never to bring her into him or press her closely against the length of him. He spent each day they were together being nothing more than an amusing and captivating companion, taking her to exclusive hotels, little waterside bistros and enchanting cafés but never for romantic candlelit dinners to whisper sweet nothings in her ear. He was playing it totally above board and utterly fairly, and it was slowly driving Maisie to distraction.

And then, suddenly, it was her last week in Italy. July and August had come and gone and the beginning of September was round the corner.

It had only really sunk in she only had a few days left that day, Maisie thought, sitting at her bedroom window as she watched the sky, a river of cinnamon, vermilion and deepest gold, display its beauty at sunset. Blaine had taken her swimming at an out of the way sandy cove he knew about and they had lit a small fire and had a barbecue for two on the beach in the afternoon. She had found the day particularly difficult, the sight of Blaine in a pair of black swimming trunks and nothing else had caused quivers in parts of her insides she hadn't even known existed. They had been lying side by side after eating their fill when the slightest chill in the warm breeze had caused her to sit up and say, with some surprise, 'I feel cold,' as she had reached for her wrap.

Blaine hadn't reacted for a moment, still lying with his eyes closed, apparently relaxed. She hadn't seen him for a full week before this day and each twenty-four hour period had seemed like an eternity. He'd explained his absence and the fact that he hadn't called in to see his parents by saying that work had been particularly busy, but Maisie had felt there was something else. Probably that he was bored with playing the attentive host to the little English girl staying with his parents.

This had seemed to be confirmed when he'd finally roused

himself, rolling on to one elbow as he'd said coolly, 'It's the beginning of September tomorrow. The summer is nearly over.'

She had been hurt by his tone although she couldn't have explained why at the time. Now, as she thought about it, she knew it was because he had been saying she would soon be going home and he didn't give a damn—but without saying it.

She knew Jenny would be sad to see her go. She and Blaine's mother had become good friends and Guiseppe treated her as one of the family. Jackie, in one of her recent phone calls, had said Blaine's father had told Roberto he thought she was a girl in a million.

A girl in a million. Maisie's mouth twisted and the tears she had been holding at bay all evening since Blaine had dropped her off home and refused to come in—for all the world as though he couldn't wait to see the back of her—flooded her eyes. Not as far as Blaine was concerned, she wasn't. And, much as she liked Jenny and Guiseppe—loved them, even—Blaine's opinion was the only one which really mattered.

Still, she'd survive. She scrubbed at her eyes with her handkerchief and turned from the window. She had four days left in Sorrento and she wasn't going to spend them weeping and wailing. Time enough for that once she was home!

Jenny and Guiseppe were out visiting friends for the evening and Liliana was staying with her sister for a few days, so for once the house was empty. Maisie hadn't expected to be home so early; she'd thought Blaine would take her out to dinner but after their conversation on the beach he had seemed to want to cut the day short and she hadn't protested. She'd rather die than beg for his company, she told herself proudly.

She didn't feel like any dinner; she felt so disturbed and

upset her stomach was churning. Ridiculous, she told herself, because nothing was any different to how it had been for weeks. And yet it seemed so somehow.

After a warm shower when she got the last of the sand out of her hair, she had an hour of pampering herself, soaking her hair in a rich conditioner before drying it, painting her toenails a bright 'Flirty Minx' red and applying a liberal amount of body lotion over every inch of skin.

It was quite dark outside now and the thought of dressing again wasn't an option. She slipped into a full-length towelling robe Jenny had given her to use while she was at the house and padded downstairs, suddenly peckish. She fixed herself a chunky sandwich using one of Liliana's recipes, which consisted of a round ciabatta filled to excess with ham, buffalo mozzarella, red pepper and salad leaves topped by beefsteak tomatoes, purposely dropping a piece of ham for Humphrey who had joined her in the kitchen. Whilst the other dogs were nervous of coming into the kitchen, having incurred Liliana's wrath on more than one occasion, Humphrey always gauged when the housekeeper wasn't around and made the most of it.

'I shall miss you,' Maisie told the little animal and when he looked dutifully soulful-eyed at the thought of their imminent parting Maisie dropped him another slice of ham as a reward. She was about to take her first bite of what was undoubtedly a jumbo sandwich when she heard the click of the front door opening. Thinking that Jenny and Guiseppe had returned early and worried that Guiseppe might be feeling ill, she put the sandwich down and hurried out into the hall.

'Oh.' She came to an abrupt halt just outside the kitchen door and her heart began to beat a violent tattoo.

'Hi.' Blaine too had stopped. In the middle of the hall.

'They're not back yet,' she said quickly.

'What?'

'Your parents. You have come to see them, haven't you?'

He stared at her for a moment. 'Not exactly.'

'Oh,' she said again. And when it didn't seem as though he was going to proffer more, she added, 'I was just making myself a sandwich. Do you want one?' She was acutely aware she was as naked as the day she was born under the robe and, although she looked perfectly decent, she didn't feel it.

'A sandwich?' he said somewhat vaguely. '*Sì*, that would be great.'

What was the matter with him? Maisie looked at him a moment more before turning and stepping into the kitchen. Once Blaine had seated himself at the kitchen table she pushed her sandwich towards him and began to make herself another one. 'I hadn't bitten it.' When he made no effort to eat, she gestured at the sandwich. 'It hasn't got my germs on it,' she said, forcing a smile. He was making her feel acutely nervous, sitting there like that just watching her.

'I would not mind your germs,' he said softly. 'Maisie, we have to talk.'

She stared at him, a piece of tomato expelling its middle on to the floor with a little plop. Using it as an excuse to break the hold of his eyes, she busied herself clearing it up, but when she was finished he was still looking at her. She pulled the robe more closely round her, knotting the belt tighter and finished making the sandwich. He still hadn't said any more.

'Do you want a drink?' she asked when the silence became deafening.

He made an impatient movement with his hand. 'If you are having one.'

She had been going to have a glass of milk but now she felt she needed something stronger. Reaching into the fridge, she pulled out a half full bottle of white wine and divided it between two glasses, placing his in front of him and then seating herself on the other side of the table. Every nerve in her body was stretched tight. She took several gulps of her wine before she said, as though he had just spoken, 'I thought we talked all day?'

'No, we did not. We have not talked since that first night at my home and you know it.'

Colour flooded into Maisie's cheeks; she could feel it. 'That was the way you wanted it,' she said with characteristic bluntness.

'That was the way I thought I wanted it.'

'And you've only just found out you didn't?' Was that what he was saying? Hope rose eternal in her bosom but she didn't dare ask him what he meant exactly. *Exactly* had got her into a lot of trouble before.

'Of course not.' He ran his hand through his hair in the gesture she had come to know meant he was agitated. Good. She wanted him to be agitated. He wouldn't be feeling half as bad as her but even a little would do.

Maisie stared at him. 'I don't understand.'

'You and me both.' Slowly Blaine exhaled. 'You breezed into my life and turned it upside down, that is the truth of it and I do not like it. I do not like it one bit.'

Put that way she was glad she hadn't asked the exactly thing. She felt a chill run through her.

'I am attracted to you, Maisie. Hell, you know that,' he said roughly.

Actually, she didn't. 'I don't.' She took another gulp of wine. 'I mean I thought you were at your house that time, but ever since… Well, you've been nice, friendly and all that, but you haven't seemed interested in me in that way.'

He looked slightly incredulous. 'You mean you haven't *guessed*?'

No. She must have left her crystal ball in England. 'It was you who wanted to be just friends,' she reminded him flatly, even though her heart was trying to exit her chest.

The hand went through the hair gain. 'I did not want it, not really, but it was necessary. I could not give you what you wanted emotionally; besides which, we did not know each other, not then. You were newly arrived in Italy; I thought perhaps this attraction would burn itself out. I thought— Hell, I do not know what I thought.'

There was something wrong here. In all the times she had imagined Blaine coming to her and telling her he'd got it wrong—and she had imagined it, more times than she'd like to remember—he hadn't had the look on his face he'd got now. In her dreams he had whispered words of undying love and togetherness and his face had been alight with desire. He hadn't looked as though the world had just ended.

'Blaine, why are you here?' she asked bluntly.

There was a long pause. 'I want you to stay in Italy,' he said, his eyes glittering. 'I do not want you to leave.' He stood up, moving round the table and pulling her to her feet as he said, 'I am going mad here. I think about you all the time; I have so many cold showers in a night it is crazy. I know we could be good together for as long as it lasts.' He kissed her, in the way she had longed for since that first night. Deeply, thrillingly, their bodies pressed hard against each other.

It would have been wonderful, but— '"For as long as it lasts"?' Maisie repeated, pushing away from him.

'I can help you find a flat here, an apartment somewhere.

And I know Mr Rossellini was serious about that offer of work. I have checked with him and you can have a job tomorrow, *sì*? We could see each other all the time.'

Maisie took a physical step backwards. 'You have asked Mr Rossellini if he would employ me?' she said faintly. He had it all worked out. He hadn't even consulted her, *asked* her, and he had it all worked out. A hot tide of rage flooded in over the crushing disappointment and hurt. Nothing had changed. He wasn't talking about togetherness or roses round the door here. Just…availability. He hadn't been able to get her out from under his skin so this was the only solution in his eyes. It wasn't even a compromise.

'*Sì*. There is no problem.'

He made the mistake of reaching for her again and Maisie slapped his hands away with enough force to stop him in his tracks, her voice trembling as she said, 'Wrong, Blaine. There's a problem all right, a huge problem. And it's all yours.'

He stood looking at her, more handsome than any man had the right to be. Maisie stared back at him and she didn't flinch when he said coldly, 'Meaning?'

'Meaning I'm not some little empty-headed doll who would be happy with the crumbs from your table; neither am I one of those career women you spoke about who can give their body to someone for a short time without thinking twice about it.'

'I know this.'

He was getting angry but she didn't care. She was angry, and she had a darn sight more reason to be than him. How dared he swan in here with the grand offer of setting her up somewhere until he got tired of her? And to actually sort out a job for her—he must have been pretty sure she would jump at the chance to stay in Italy to be near him. 'No, you don't know it,' she said furiously, 'or you wouldn't be here now saying what you have.' All he had put her through the last weeks, all the emotional—not to mention the physical—torment, and he thought he could come up with this offer and have her falling at his feet in gratitude? *What did he think she was?*

'You have misunderstood me.'

'No, you laid it out very clearly and I understood every word,' she shot back tensely. 'You know I like you, that much is clear, and you thought I would agree to being a temporary fixture in your life, a ship that passes ever so slowly in the night. Wrong. I don't do one-night or even a hundred-night stands. Laugh if you want, but when I give myself to a man it will be because I know it is going to be for ever, the whole caboodle. Ring, togetherness, children, the lot.'

She saw his eyes narrow as he registered the words. There was a sharp eternal pause and Maisie could hear her heart-beat drumming in her ears.

'You were engaged to be married,' he said slowly. 'This Jeff... You must have slept with him.'

'There is no must about it.' She didn't care that he would think she was the most pathetic creature on earth, that she was so far removed from the type of woman he had been associ-ating with as to come from another planet. And she sure as blazes wasn't going to apologise for her virginity either—it had been her decision to stay that way and it wasn't as if she hadn't had offers.

'But that night.' He was speaking like someone who was wading through treacle. 'You would have slept with me that night.'

'Then you must be my Achilles heel,' she said tightly. She didn't trust herself to say anything more; the intensity of Blaine's gaze was making it difficult to think.

He stood staring at her for what seemed like an eternity. 'You want me,' he said expressionlessly. 'You know you do. You have just said it. What would be so wrong in us being together and enjoying each other for a time? You like my parents and they like you, you find Italy a good place to be.'

He just didn't get it. Maisie tried to keep her voice steady when she said, 'You would be breaking all your rules, wouldn't you? The ones about not taking your woman of the moment home to Mother or, more to the point, Liliana?'

'I would break rules for you, Maisie.'

But only to a point. Only to a point. She had to say it. It was the only way to make him see. The only way to finally end this affair which had never been an affair. 'I don't want you, Blaine.' She saw him blink. 'I love you and that is quite a different thing. If I agreed to what you have proposed it would kill me. Can you understand that? Think of me as the original clingy woman if you want, if that makes it easier to see where I am coming from; I don't care. The truth is I love you and I would want it all. Togetherness. For ever. Nothing less. Children. Little Blaines and Maisies. Knowing I can trust you never to look at another woman and you knowing you can trust me. Living together, loving together, growing old together.'

She took a deep breath, knowing she was finishing it for good. 'Absolute roses round the door finale, in fact.' She tried to smile but her mouth was trembling too much. 'Nothing less would do for me where you're concerned.'

'That is impossible.' He was as white as a sheet. 'I have told you how I feel. That would be impossible for me.'

'Then all we can do is to remain friends.'

'We could never be just friends.'

It was so sharp that Humphrey, who had disappeared under

the table with Blaine's arrival, growled a warning. He wasn't going to have anyone hurt his favourite human. 'Maybe not,' Maisie said steadily, 'but that's how it is.'

'I have offered you more than I have offered any other woman since Francesca died.' There was a furious glint in his eyes.

'You offered the others nothing,' she said shakily, 'and what you offer me isn't enough.'

'I can't do what you want, don't you understand?' he groaned, his voice softer now. 'I'm offering you all I'm capable of right now, Maisie. I don't know about the future, who does?'

'I don't buy that.' She smiled sadly. 'I know I could love you for ever, you see, so that makes a difference.'

'And yet you are prepared to walk out of my life? To leave Italy for ever, to leave *me* for ever?'

Oh, he was good, she had to give him that. He knew just how to twist the knife so it really hurt. 'Yes.'

'What sort of love is that?' he said flatly.

She shrugged. 'My sort, I suppose. Because I know if I stayed it would be wrong. I would start becoming the type of female I've always despised, the kind who goes through their man's pockets to see if there's something there that indicates they're involved with someone else. The sort who if they find something don't say anything because they don't want to rock the boat, because they're prepared to take even a little rather than lose the whole thing. That's where compromise leads. And eventually I would be a different person and you wouldn't want me anyway. I love you, Blaine, more than you will ever be loved by anyone else, but I won't let you destroy me.'

'I would never do that,' he said, clearly appalled, reaching out and tugging her into him. He crushed her mouth beneath his and for a moment the temptation to give in, to say she would be his, was so strong she could taste it. She loved him and she would make him love her. Being near him, seeing him, loving him, she would become such a part of his life he wouldn't want to let her go.

And then reality kicked in. Love was either there or it wasn't; if nothing else, she had learnt that over the last months. He had accused her of turning his life upside down—he'd had hers spinning almost from the first time she had met him. He was the last person she would have chosen to love—a handsome, wealthy Adonis who would attract any woman within a radius of fifty miles. An Adonis with massive hangups into the bargain, who readily admitted he wanted women who were content to give him what he wanted and then depart with a smile and a kiss.

If she could have chosen a man to love it would have been a down-to-earth, ordinary, well-adjusted individual, the type of guy who would have been over the moon to put a ring on her finger and more than content to have a quiverful of children and a home filled with cats and dogs. A man like Jeff—without the Camellia bit. The sort of man who would be lost in a crowd. But she would have loved him and he her, and that would have been all that mattered.

But love wasn't like that. It didn't fit into a neat little parcel. She loved Blaine Morosini and that was the end of it. But he didn't love her. He *wanted* her, but he didn't love her. His need was a thing of the flesh, nothing more.

Maisie drew on every bit of strength in her mind and body and pushed Blaine away. 'I think you had better leave,' she said quietly.

'You do not mean that.'

'Yes, I do.'

'No, think clearly. What we have, it is extraordinary. You feel this as well as I do. I have slept with women but never have I felt this…' He shook his head. 'You need me as much as I need you, admit it.'

'You need me. I love you. All the difference in the world. Goodbye, Blaine.'

For a moment she thought he was going to argue some more. Then he just turned and walked out of the house. Just like that. Without even a goodbye.

She heard the front door bang with enough force to crack the plaster but apart from murmuring, 'Not so cool tonight, then,' she remained immobile. He'd gone. She couldn't quite believe it. Only now did she admit she had been hoping this would turn out like some Hollywood film. But not one where the two of them end up alone. Not that. She burst into tears.

She cried until there were no more tears left and then finished both glasses of wine, throwing the sandwiches into the bin. She now had the sort of headache that—mercifully—prevented any coherent thought and, after taking a couple of painkillers from the box of medicines Liliana kept in a high cupboard in the kitchen, she wearily made her way back to her room before Jenny and Guiseppe arrived home. The perfect end to a perfect day would have been trying to explain her ten-rounds-with-Mike-Tyson face to Blaine's parents.

When Humphrey jumped on her bed a minute or so later—something which was totally against every rule in the house because no animals were allowed upstairs—she made no attempt to push the little dog away. He crept up against her, licking the salt tears and snuffling as he pushed his head against hers. He must have followed her up the stairs and nipped in the room before she closed the door, Maisie thought, reaching out an arm and drawing the little animal to her. She suddenly realised it wasn't only Blaine who was going to break her heart when she left Italy. She loved this little dog and she knew he loved her.

She didn't expect to fall asleep, not with her life in ruins and little men with nasty great hammers beating away at a gong in her head, but gradually, with the warmth of Humphrey's furry body and the knowledge she wasn't totally alone, she felt herself beginning to drift away. She went into the blanketing darkness thankfully. If she could just sleep for ever, that would be fine by her. That was the way she felt. And she wasn't going to apologise for it either.

CHAPTER ELEVEN

THE old adage about tomorrow being another day could be taken two ways, Maisie decided, when she surfaced the next morning. She supposed its original meaning—things getting better and all that—might be true for some people in some situations. For her, right now, all it meant was that this was the first day of the disaster that was the rest of her life.

She said as much to Humphrey, who at some time during the night had worked himself into a snug bundle lying in the crook of her bent legs and was now surveying her with bright brown eyes. He didn't answer, but then she hadn't expected him to.

'And now I've got to smuggle you downstairs somehow,' she told him. 'or we'll both be in for it.' He wagged his tail, tongue lolling, for all the world as though he was laughing at her. She sighed. 'If it wasn't for putting you through the horror of quarantine, I'd take you back with me. Do you know that?'

She sat up as she spoke and he immediately rolled over for his tummy to be stroked. Maisie smiled. 'Fusspot,' she said huskily.

They both made it downstairs without anyone being any the wiser, and once Maisie had fed the dogs and cats she set about taking a tray of coffee, orange juice and croissants up to Jenny and Guiseppe. She had done this every morning since Liliana had been away—it was the housekeeper's normal routine—and although Jenny had protested the first day she had given in with good grace when Maisie had said she wanted to do it.

'You've been so generous to me,' Maisie had said to Blaine's mother. 'Let me at least do little things like this for you.' Although Maisie had objected, Jenny had insisted on paying her handsomely for every week she had been in Italy.

When she knocked on the door of the master bedroom suite Jenny came to the door to take the tray like she usually did, beaming at her as she said, 'Oh, Maisie, I'm going to miss you, and I don't just mean because you do things like this. Why don't you stay for a bit longer, but for a real holiday this time?'

She had mentioned this before but Maisie had demurred. Now she said, 'I've had a real holiday, Jenny; that's why I feel guilty for taking any money from you. It's been wonderful, just wonderful, but I must get home and see about getting a job and somewhere to live. I don't want to do that in the middle of an English winter.'

'Blaine will miss you,' Jenny put in slyly.

Maisie looked at her. She had thought Blaine's parents accepted that she and Blaine were just friends. Now she wondered. Colouring slightly, she said, 'He'll probably be relieved he's off the hook about showing me around all the time.'

'Don't you believe it.' Maisie watched the expression on Jenny's face change. 'Maisie, I know my son is a hard man to understand but he hasn't always been like he is now. Once he was so open, so—'

'He's told me about Francesca,' Maisie said hurriedly when she saw Jenny was struggling for words.

'He has?' Jenny's eyes widened in surprise. 'But he never talks about her, not even to his father and me.'

Realising that Jenny might draw quite the wrong conclusions from Blaine confiding in her, Maisie said awkwardly, 'I think it was because he wanted me to know we could only ever be friends, Jenny.'

Jenny took a moment to digest this. Then she said, 'If I had known he'd talked with you I would have spoken of it all, Maisie, but he made it very clear at the time to Guiseppe and me it was a private thing he didn't want discussed. Out of respect for his feelings, we haven't spoken of it with anyone.'

'No, I understand perfectly.' She and Jenny had talked about a lot of things over the time she had been in Italy; she had shared how her father had left and that she and her mother had never got on, besides explaining about Jeff, and now Maisie realised Blaine's mother was probably feeling awkward herself. 'I truly wouldn't have expected you to discuss Blaine's personal life, Jenny. If he wanted to do that, that's one thing, but someone else—even you, his mother—that's different.'

Jenny smiled, her voice soft as she said, 'You're such a lovely girl, Maisie. So understanding.'

She didn't feel like a lovely girl and as far as Blaine was concerned she didn't understand a thing. Maisie forced herself to smile back. 'Thank you.'

'It was so tragic at the time,' Jenny said quietly, 'especially as Francesca had been battling against the mental illness for years.'

Maisie remembered that Blaine's parents weren't aware of the true facts or how things had really been between Blaine and his wife, and now she felt even more uncomfortable.

'Blaine changed dramatically but then no one thought that was surprising. Francesca was so young, so beautiful, with all her life ahead of her; it was bound to hit him hard.'

Maisie nodded.

'And now…' Jenny shook her head. 'He has closed in on himself, become totally self-reliant. I thought this would be a phase which would pass but it has been a long time now. Of course there are women.'

She saw Maisie's look of surprise and smiled sadly. 'I am not Liliana,' she said softly. 'I love my son, I would lay down my life for him, but I do not have rose-coloured spectacles where he's concerned. He is a man and he is very human, like his father. There would have to be women. Work would not be the be all and end all for Blaine, he's not made like that. If he found the right one then he would not look at another woman, I know this too. Guiseppe loved his first wife and he was completely faithful to Luisa while she lived. When he met me, it was the same. I have never had cause to doubt him.'

Guiseppe's voice calling from the bedroom broke into the conversation, and Maisie had never been more thankful for something in her life. She appreciated Jenny speaking so openly to her but the conversation was definitely on the painful lines.

'I'm sure Blaine will meet the right woman at some point,' she said, because Jenny needed to hear it. She just hoped by then she would have picked up the pieces of her life. Either that or Jackie didn't tell her about it when it happened. 'You go and eat now. I'll see you later.'

Once in the kitchen she busied herself with various household chores that Liliana usually did, glad of something to do. She was going to keep busy for the next two or three days before she left, she told herself firmly. Fill every moment. No moping. The original plan had been that Blaine would pick her up and take her to the airport; now she rather thought she would pay for a taxi. She could explain things to Jenny by saying her flight was in the morning and she didn't want to take Blaine away from his work. It was a weak excuse as excuses went but it would have to do. She would book her flight today, get herself organised, arrange for the taxi, everything. It was time to go. High time.

She followed through on the plan during the day, leaving a message on Blaine's mobile phone explaining that because her flight was a late morning one she didn't want to disrupt his day and had therefore organised a taxi to take her to the airport. She thanked him for the lovely days out and meals they'd enjoyed and finished the message by saying politely she was sure they would see each other some time in the future when he visited his brother's family. At the same time she made a mental note to be sure to ask Jackie if there was any possibility of Blaine being there if she went to her friend's home again. A meeting wasn't an option as far as she was concerned.

She filled the day to the brim with activity, falling into bed that night too tired to think. Blaine hadn't phoned back, but then she hadn't expected him to. She hoped he would at least have the sensitivity to leave things as they were and avoid any more traumatic arguments.

The next two days passed with equal uneventfulness, and on the evening before the morning she was due to leave Maisie telephoned her mother. She had spoken to her twice since she had been in Italy and both times she had finished the call wondering why she'd bothered to phone in the first place. This time was no different.

'Hallo, Mum, it's me,' Maisie said with determined cheerfulness when she heard her mother's voice on the end of the line.

'I'm just ringing to let you know I'm coming back tomorrow and that I shall be staying at Sue's flat for a while. OK?'

'While you look for a job? Well, let's hope you find one fairly quickly, but I doubt it. I doubt it very much.'

Great, thanks a bunch. 'I'm not worried,' Maisie said brightly. 'I'm sure I'll find something.'

'Huh. I've heard plenty say that and then come a cropper.'

Not that you're wishing it on me or anything to prove a point, of course. 'Anyway, I just thought I'd let you know I'll be back in England. I'll ring you when I can pop and see you for a day or so.'

'I won't hold my breath for that.'

The same old sayings, the same old moaning. And it wasn't as if her mother even really *cared*. 'Goodbye, Mum.'

'Aren't you going to ask me how I am?'

'How are you?'

'All right, no thanks to you, though. Gadding about all over the place at your age and without a job or home to come back to. I can't believe you're my daughter, Maisie, I tell you straight.'

'Perhaps there was a mix-up at the hospital when I was born.'

'See? You don't take anything seriously. Just like your father. He needed a rocket up his posterior to even get up in the morning, just like you.'

She didn't actually need to take this. Maisie stared at the telephone, picturing her mother's tight-lipped face and iron eyes. 'My father was a very clever man and a hard worker,' she said steadily, 'and you know it. If I'm like him in any way at all then I thank my lucky stars for it. If you want to see anything of me in the future, please remember I loved him and I won't stand to hear him maligned by you or any of the crew you associate with. I'll let you think about that—whether you want to see me again—and I'll ring some time when I am back. Goodbye.'

She put down the phone with a shaking hand and promptly burst into tears, but once she'd had a little cry and dried her eyes she felt better. That had been waiting to be said for years and she didn't doubt for a minute it would cause a rift between not only her mother and herself but the rest of the relations in the north. She was really on her own now. No job, no home, no family.

She took a deep breath and then expelled the air slowly. New start then. In every sense of the word. Probably not a bad thing. And, thinking about it, she perhaps wouldn't stay with Sue after all or hang around London. She fancied moving somewhere slower and more beautiful. Yorkshire, perhaps, or the Lake District. And if she couldn't get a veterinary nurse position, then she would do anything—working on the till at a supermarket or something—until she could. She had enough money behind her now to rent a small place for several months; she could do it. She nodded to the thought.

She would build a new life for herself. It wouldn't be the life she ideally wanted because it wouldn't have Blaine in it, and having met him she doubted she would ever be even slightly interested in anyone else, but given time she would adjust. She would have to because she wasn't about to lie down and die. There were worse things than going through life single—she couldn't actually think of any right at this moment, but there were.

When Maisie awoke the following morning it was raining. In fact it wasn't just raining, it was absolutely bucketing down, she thought, as she gazed out of the window into a sodden landscape. Entirely appropriate for her mood, but a surprise because there had only been the odd light shower through the summer.

She continued to stand in her nightie looking out over the scene which had become so familiar over the last months, her stomach churning at the thought of leaving.

Jenny hadn't queried her announcement as to why Blaine wasn't taking her to the airport, although she had tried to insist that she would drive her there. Maisie had overridden this, insisting she'd already booked the taxi and that she would really rather not do goodbyes at the airport. 'They are such emotive places,' she'd said to Jenny, 'and I don't want to cry in public. You know?'

She didn't have to rush downstairs that morning because Liliana had arrived home late the night before and would be seeing to Jenny and Guiseppe's tray. Nevertheless, she showered and dressed quickly—having packed the night before—and went down to see to the animals' food. Whether Humphrey sensed she was leaving she didn't know, but certainly the little animal wasn't his usual bouncy self, his whiskered face woebegone as he ate his food.

She put a plastic raincoat over her head and dashed down to the horses in the stable, staying there for quite a while as she made her goodbyes. Ithel gave her a soft-nosed farewell, pushing his head into her hand and letting her stroke his smooth back. He wasn't in the least bit skittish with her as he was with everyone else, even Jenny, and Maisie was sure it was because somehow the foal knew she had been involved in the fight for his life.

By the time she got back to the house everyone was up, and after forcing down a couple of pieces of toast she went to her room and made sure everything was in her bags. Her hair had got slightly wispy and curly in the damp air; she pulled it into a high ponytail on the back of her head and stared at herself in the mirror. 'This is it, girl.' Her nerves had become more taut as the morning had progressed; now they were as tightly coiled as a spring. 'Last few minutes saying goodbye and then you're off.'

She lugged her case and bags downstairs, getting a scolding from Jenny in the process, who had told her to call her so she could help, and, steeling herself, began her goodbyes. One day when she had been out with Blaine she had bought little presents for Jenny, Guiseppe and Liliana. Now she gave the two women the beautiful handmade shawls she had for them, Guiseppe receiving his bottle of his favourite liqueur with gruff thanks.

'And something for you.' She bent down to Humphrey, who had barely left her side all morning, earning himself harsh words from Liliana in the process when he had tried to creep upstairs to her. She put the soft leather collar complete with a little engraved medal with his name and the house telephone number round Humphrey's neck after taking off his old frayed one. He licked her hand as she did so and it was only then that she cried.

This set Jenny and Liliana off and sent Guiseppe into his study declaring there was nothing to cry about. Maisie would come and see them again, wouldn't she? This wasn't really goodbye, was it? Next year she must come for a holiday and stay for as long as she wanted.

None of them heard the key turning in the lock of the front door in all the commotion, and it was only when Liliana cried, 'Blaine! I did not know you were coming,' that Jenny and Maisie's heads turned too, Guiseppe reappearing.

'I have come to take Maisie to the airport.' His voice was steady and even, his face deadpan and his clothes immaculate. If it wasn't for the fact that he looked exhausted, the bags under his eyes indicating he hadn't slept properly in days, Maisie would have vehemently protested.

As it was she said, 'Thank you, but didn't you get my message? I've ordered a taxi,' as she hastily dabbed at her eyes with her handkerchief. Wonderful. His last sight of her would be with a blotchy face and red nose. Not quite the lasting memory she wanted him to carry.

'I've cancelled it.'

She stared at him, completely taken aback and feeling like a shock wave had just gone over her head. She wanted to be angry at his high-handedness and refuse to go with him, but with his parents and Liliana watching she could hardly do that. Besides which, she didn't feel angry. She felt so bereft and emotional that all she wanted to do was sit and howl. Like Humphrey.

'What on earth is the matter with that dog?' As the sound which had been steadily gathering volume after starting with whimpers after Maisie had fastened the new collar registered on Guiseppe, he cast a startled look at Humphrey.

'It is because Maisie is leaving,' Jenny answered, but with her eyes on her son. 'He does not want her to go. He knows he is losing something irreplaceable.'

Blaine's eyes flickered to his mother's for the briefest of moments and a look passed between them. Then he said, 'He will get used to it in time.'

'I doubt that.' Jenny's voice was sad. 'He does not give his heart easily.'

Blaine turned away. 'Are these your bags?' he said, asking the obvious as he picked up Maisie's case and other belongings before walking out to the car parked on the drive.

Jenny took Maisie's hands in hers in a tight grip. 'Be happy,' she said in a low voice. 'And promise you'll come and see us again.'

She couldn't. Maisie tried to smile but it was wobbly. 'I hope Humphrey is all right.'

'So do I.' Jenny's grip became tighter. 'I didn't know,' she said softly. 'I'm so sorry, Maisie.'

Guiseppe, in typical male fashion, was standing looking at them with a puzzled expression on his face as he tried to follow a conversation which had become incomprehensible. Liliana had bustled off into the kitchen, returning with a bag holding sandwiches, fruit, cakes and chocolate bars. 'For the journey,' she said, handing it to Maisie. It would have done credit for an expedition to the North Pole.

After bending down and fussing Humphrey one last time, Maisie followed Blaine out to the car, the others coming to stand in the doorway of the house. The rain was still hammering down and, as she slid into the Ferrari and Blaine shut the door, Maisie felt as though she was looking at them all through a veil of teardrops as the rain coursed down the windows of the car. It was entirely appropriate.

They didn't speak until they had exited the drive and were on their way. Then Blaine passed her a crisp white handkerchief to replace her soggy one. 'You didn't really think I would let you leave without saying goodbye, did you, *mia piccola*?' he said softly without glancing at her, his eyes intent on the road as the windscreen wipers laboured to take the water away.

'It would have been better,' she whispered when she could find her voice. Certainly less painful. For her.

'Nothing about this situation could be better.' He raked his hair, which comforted her a fraction. 'I have not slept since we last parted, do you know this?'

She wasn't going to say she was sorry because she wasn't. It surprised her that he had been sufficiently disturbed to be unable to sleep but she had to admit to feeling glad. Nasty probably, but she'd never pretended to be perfect. Not being called Camellia, she didn't have to. 'What do you want me to say?' she prevaricated.

'That you have changed your mind would be nice.' It was a growl. 'But there is no hope of that. Impossible woman. Impossible situation.'

'We've already done this to death.' She couldn't go through it all again. Whatever he was feeling, and she had to accept he was feeling more than she had thought he would from the look of him, it wasn't enough. He hadn't come to tell her he couldn't live without her. He never would. Because it wasn't true.

'*Sì*, I know.' He breathed deeply and for a few moments the silence crackled. 'And I did not come today to fight.'

'Why did you come?'

'Because I could not stay away,' he said simply. 'I could not let you leave in a taxi and without saying goodbye properly. The last time we saw each other—' he banged his fist on the steering wheel, making her jump slightly '—it was a mess, was it not?'

'In a way.' She tried to steady her voice. 'But it was honest. We were both honest. What I feel for you is different from what you feel for me, and we both want different things for the future too. It's better to have everything out in the open. I have never believed in sweeping things under the carpet.'

'My honest brave Maisie.' It was said in a quieter tone, more rueful than angry.

She turned to look blindly out of the window. This was almost more than she could bear. After a few minutes she said, 'I shall miss Humphrey. He's a dear little dog. And your parents and Liliana, of course.'

He nodded but said nothing and they continued to the airport through the streaming countryside, the atmosphere within the car tenser by the mile. Maisie found herself silently praying for the strength to say goodbye properly when the time came. She didn't want to weep and wail and cling hold of him although she knew that was how she would feel. But she had to leave with dignity. After all that had passed between them and the way she had bared her heart to him and been rejected, she had to be able to hold her head up when they said farewell.

When they reached the airport she said, 'You don't have to come in with me. Just drop me outside and I'll be fine.'

'Do not be ridiculous.' It was final.

After parking the Ferrari he took her case and bags, leaving Maisie with just her handbag, and they walked into the airport. It had stopped raining minutes before and now the air held the peculiarly distinctive smell of rain on concrete which had been baked by the sun. Maisie knew she would never be able to smell the aftermath of a summer storm without reliving this acutely painful moment.

After checking in, Blaine insisted on buying her a coffee she didn't want. His face was closed and guarded as they sat sipping their drinks and Maisie didn't have a clue as to what was going on behind the smooth mask he'd adopted. But it was helping her to remain strong and that was the main thing. If he had started trying to persuade her to stay again or had spoken words of desire or held her, this would have been so much harder.

And then it was time to go through to board the plane. He walked with her as far as he was allowed and then handed her the bag Liliana had given her for the journey and which had not been put in the hold. Maisie was trembling violently—she couldn't help it—but a kind of numb acceptance had settled on her mind, which enabled her to say, 'I shall miss you. Take care of yourself.' And then she handed him the package she had been about to give Jenny to give to him before he had walked in the door.

'What is this?' He stared down at the small parcel.

'Just a little thank you for being such a wonderful escort.' Good. Well done. Keep it up and in just a few more seconds you can exit his life with grace. 'Don't open it now; I'd be embarrassed.'

'Thank you.' His voice was hoarse and a muscle was working in his jaw. 'It was not necessary, but thank you.'

Maisie nodded jerkily. 'Goodbye, then.' She reached up and kissed him on one cheek before stepping back smartly. She just could not do a hug. They would have to prise her off him kicking and screaming if she attempted a hug.

She guessed he'd realised she was at breaking-point because he did not try to kiss her or take her in his arms. They simply stared at each other for what seemed a long, long time before she turned and walked away. She looked back at the last moment and saw him standing very still and alone, the package held in his hands as though he was cupping an injured bird.

And then she walked out of sight.

CHAPTER TWELVE

RIGHT up until the moment when the plane rose into the air Maisie was hoping something would happen. That somehow Blaine would board the aircraft and demand she leave with him. Daft, she knew, in these days of heightened security, but she still couldn't help hoping. Or that she would turn round and see him sitting somewhere. He would say he had bought a ticket at the last moment because finally he knew she meant everything to him. Or there would be a message sent via the control tower. Maisie Burns, will you marry Blaine Morosini? Something like that.

Of course it didn't happen. Because this was real life, Maisie thought miserably as the plane rose into the air and up into the clouds. Not a film or a book where a happy ending was guaranteed. Besides, Blaine was too big a character for a film. He would dominate all the other actors to the point where there would be an uprising.

The shadow of a smile touched her mouth at the thought. No, this was real life all right and she had to get on with it. On her own. Oh, she did so wish she wasn't going to Sue's but to a place of her own. Somewhere where she could lick her wounds in private and be as miserable as she needed to be.

She felt awful about that thought when Sue met her at the

airport, all welcome-the-weary-traveller. It felt strange to be standing on English soil again. No, not strange. Awful. She felt as though she had been torn away from her real home and deposited in a foreign place, which was pretty weird when you thought about it.

'So, how was Italy?' Sue sported a new streaked and carefully tousled hairdo and looked slimmer than ever. 'Good, was it? Don't tell me you met a handsome Italian hunk and you're going to have his babies or I'll spit.'

'No such luck.' Despite doing her best to sound flippant and amused, Maisie heard her voice crack. The next moment she had surprised them both by bursting into tears, right in the middle of Arrivals.

'Oh, kiddo. What is it? Don't cry.'

Maisie remembered why Sue was one of her two best friends when the other woman rose to the occasion, putting her arms round her, careless of interested passers-by, and hugging her tight. It took a real friend not to mind when your nose and eyes were expelling bodily fluids all over her Valentino jacket. 'I... I can't...'

'Come on.' Sue seized her case and one of her bags, leaving Maisie with a small overnight bag and the one Liliana had pressed on her and which she hadn't even looked in. For once food had been the last thing on her mind through the torturous journey home when she had decided life, as she knew it, was over. 'We're going straight back to my place and you can have a long hot bath while I get something to eat, and then you can tell me all about it.'

Maisie found herself whisked out of the airport and into Sue's smart little car before she'd had time to catch her breath. Once they'd arrived at her friend's small but charming pad in Kensington, Sue deposited her things in the spare bedroom and then ran her a bath with an oil, which smelt as though it cost hundreds of pounds a sniff. Which it probably did, knowing Sue.

Maisie spent some time in the bath, mainly because she was dreading having to go over the whole sorry business again. But Sue, having got the bit between her teeth, would be content with nothing less. As it was, once she was ensconced in one of Sue's old bathrobes—at least it was meant to be old but as far as Maisie could see it was almost brand new and certainly better than anything she possessed—and they started eating, she found it something of a relief to finally unburden herself. She didn't tell Sue everything, though— Blaine had told her the details about his life with Francesca in confidence and she couldn't share that with anyone. But she didn't hold back on how she felt.

For once Sue was speechless when Maisie came to a finish. She stared at her for a few moments. Then she said, 'The rotten so-and-so. He might have known you weren't like one of those other women.'

Maisie blinked. Startled, she realised that in not telling Sue all of it she might have put Blaine in a bad light. 'It's not really his fault,' she said quickly. 'It's just that after his wife being ill for years and then dying like that he doesn't want commitment.'

Sue snorted. 'Maisie, don't do your understanding thing again. Get angry.'

'What?'

'Right from when your father left you found excuses for him. And for how your mother behaves. When Gary turned out to be a jerk you didn't get angry and said it was for the best and all that, and even *Jeff*.' Sue paused for breath, shaking her head. 'I mean, lots of women in your position would have keyed his car at the very least. Or thrown away half of the records at the surgery when no one was looking. Or painted something very rude on the pavement in front of his house.'

Maisie was gazing at Sue with something like admiration. 'I never thought of any of that,' she said truthfully.

'I *know*. That's what I mean. You're too *nice*. And you're even worried about how that little dog, Harold, will cope now you've gone.'

'Humphrey.'

'Humphrey, then. You ought to be thinking purely of yourself. Don't you *see*?'

'I am thinking of myself. That's why I'm going to move to Yorkshire and have a complete change. And I did tell my mother what I thought of her. Don't forget about that.'

'I suppose that's a start.' Sue was staring at her with something like despair on her face. 'Maisie, promise me one thing, all right? If Jackie's uncle comes sniffing around pretending he's had time to consider and suggesting you go back there to see how things work out, promise me you'll tell him to take a hike. If he really cared about you he wouldn't have let you go. You know that, don't you?'

If this was meant to be cheering her up and helping, it wasn't. Maisie nodded.

'He was trying it on. All along. Playing games. And when he found out you were, well, you know—'

'A virgin?'

'Well, yes, it probably became more of a challenge. Some men are like that. I wouldn't be at all surprised if he just *happens* to come over to England and just *happens* to bump into you and—'

'Sue.' Maisie's tone of voice stopped her friend in her tracks. 'I know you're trying to be helpful and in a way you've got a point, but Blaine isn't anything like you think he is. OK? And, trust me on this, he won't come looking for me. So can we leave it now and talk about something else?'

Sue stared at her for a moment. 'Fancy some chocolate cake for afters? It's that one you really love with bits of flake and fresh cream.'

Maisie didn't but she wouldn't have said so for all the world. Which probably bore out at least some of what Sue had been saying.

By the time the two friends said goodnight and retired to their respective rooms Maisie knew she wanted to leave London as soon as possible. Perhaps even tomorrow? Lovely though Sue had been, Maisie felt she needed to be somewhere where no one knew her history, where the deepest conversation she'd have with someone would be about the weather. Some folk might term it running away and maybe it was, but she didn't care. It was what she needed right now and that was that. If it didn't work out she could always come back to London and begin again. And if it worked out well, she wouldn't. Simple. About the only thing in her life that was.

She sat down on the bed, fighting the urge to cry, and it was then that her eyes focused on Liliana's bag. The food! She felt a guilty dart that she hadn't at least sorted through and put what could be salvaged in Sue's fridge. Walking across the room, she lifted the bag on to the small dressing table and took out the contents, and there, right at the bottom where it must have slipped down during the journey, was a little box tied with a ribbon.

A present from Liliana? Oh, bless her, Maisie thought, flipping over the little card attached to the box.

I hope in time the memories this evokes will be happy ones. We're both going to miss you. Blaine.

Her hands shaking and her eyes already filling with tears, Maisie undid the ribbon and opened the little box. She took out the beautifully worked little dog that was Humphrey right down to the funny little clump of hair under his chin and stared at it as the tears dripped off her face. Blaine must have had it specially made—it was too like Humphrey to be a co-incidence. The sculpture sat in her hand, looking up at her with soulful eyes, and her heart broke.

She walked across to the bed again and sat sobbing and shaking for long minutes before she tried to pull herself together. What had Blaine thought of his present? she wondered as she wiped her eyes and blew her nose after putting the little dog safely on the dressing table. She had seen the small painting on one of their days out in a shop next door to the restaurant where Blaine chose to eat, and under the pretext of going to the ladies' cloakroom had crept out and bought it. It had been by a local artist of high renown and very expensive, but the Mediterranean villa had been evocative of summer days and mellow evenings, the children playing in the sunlit courtyard and the woman standing in the doorway watching them exquisitely painted. But it had been the roses round the door of the villa that had caught her attention.

Maisie sniffed and wiped her eyes again. At the time she had bought it with a tongue-in-cheek attitude, hoping he would take it in the spirit it was meant and see the joke. Now it was too poignant to even think about. Especially after her little sculpture.

She climbed into bed, curling up into a little ball under the covers and knowing sleep was a million miles away. Was

Blaine lying awake thinking of her? She hoped he was. She hoped he was as miserable as her and that he didn't get over her departure from his life too quickly, even if it was lust and not love on his side. That might mean her love for him was a bit egotistical and selfish, but if half of what Sue had said was true she was due a bit of putting herself first anyway. Not that she particularly wanted to—she'd love Blaine to be part of her life so she could put him first. First, second and third.

She sniffed, reaching for her handkerchief. It was going to be another long night...

The next day at three o'clock in the afternoon Maisie stepped off the train and stood gazing about her. The Yorkshire air was bracing. Not exactly below zero, but definitely bracing. She pulled her jacket collar up round her neck and picked up her case, walking out of the station.

The very nice taxi driver recommended a bed and breakfast when Maisie asked; it was his sister's place, he said, but for all that it was definitely second to none. Later that evening Maisie phoned Sue and Jackie and told them where she was and that she was fine. She wasn't and they all knew that, but some things were better left unsaid.

She spent a week in the bed and breakfast before moving into a tiny one-bedroomed flat on the ground floor of an old terraced house in Thirsk. The town was very English with its cobbled market place, eighteenth-century inns and old buildings, and that suited her. She could do English. It was any reminder of foreign climes she couldn't handle.

When, within days, she had found a job at a veterinary practice which was practically on her doorstep, she knew someone up there was looking after her. Everything had fallen into place with remarkable ease and she knew she ought to be grateful, but the ton weight on her heart made it difficult to feel anything much at all.

But that would pass, she reassured herself each night. She had arranged the delivery of her few bits of furniture and personal belongings from the friend who had been storing them for her, she had a much nicer little home than she'd had in London, she had money in the bank—thanks to Jenny's generosity, and she was again doing the job she loved on a salary she could live on. It was enough. It would have to be enough.

She had been living in Yorkshire for nearly six weeks when Jackie rang her one night to say she and Sue were coming up for the weekend and intended to take her out for a slap-up meal. 'We're bringing sleeping bags and will spin a coin to see who sleeps on the sofa and who has the floor,' Jackie said cheerfully when Maisie warned her there was only one single bed in the place. 'It'll be fun.'

Maisie didn't protest too hard. Everyone had been very friendly at work and she had already had a couple of invites to go out with the other two nurses, who were both young and fancy free, but it wasn't the same as being with Sue and Jackie. She did warn Jackie to bring winter woollies, though. It was only the last week of October but they had already had several white frosts and even a sprinkling of snow the day before.

Sue and Jackie arrived in Sue's little car at eleven o'clock on Saturday morning, having been up at the crack of dawn for the two hundred and forty odd mile journey—as Jackie wearily informed her. Jackie had wanted to come by train but Sue loved driving and rarely had the chance to put her smart little car through its paces.

'Come on in and I'll make a coffee.' Maisie pulled them

into the kitchen as she spoke. The house had been converted in such a way that she had her own separate front door accessed from the narrow front garden. The other three flats—one each on the first and second floors and then a loft conversion—had a communal key to a door leading to stairs from which the respective flats were approached. 'We'll get your stuff in later.'

After hugs all round the three of them had just sat down with a cup of coffee and slice of cheesecake—at least Sue and Jackie had sat down on the two stools the kitchen boasted and Maisie was perched half on the worktop, one leg on the floor and the other dangling—when a knock came at the door. 'Apart from you two, I haven't had one other person come to the door since I've been here and now there's three in one morning,' Maisie said, sliding off the worktop and walking across to the door.

She pulled it open and then the world stopped spinning and everything was flung into space. There was a moment of utter silence and then Blaine said softly, 'Hallo, Maisie.'

He was real, then. He wasn't a product of her fevered imagination. She stared at him but she still couldn't speak or move. She heard a scramble behind her and then Sue's voice saying, 'I don't believe your cheek! How dare you come here?'

Then Jackie babbling, 'I didn't give him the address, Sue. I promise. We agreed, didn't we?' And then they were both at her elbow.

'Shut the door!' This was from Sue.

But it was only when her friend tried to grab the handle that Maisie found the strength to say, 'Don't, Sue. Look, would you two please take your coffees through to the sitting room for a minute?' And to Blaine, 'Come in.'

Sue groaned. 'Don't ask him *in*, Maisie,' she implored,

before turning to Jackie and saying, 'How *could* you? I mean I know he's your uncle and everything, but how could you after we agreed we wouldn't say?'

'She didn't say.' Blaine was talking to Sue but he hadn't taken his eyes from Maisie's white face. 'Her mother let slip you were both going away for the weekend and I put two and two together. I followed Jackie to your house last night and then waited outside until you left this morning.'

'All night?' Jackie squeaked.

'All night, and then I followed you. It wasn't difficult.'

The icy wind blew a quiff of hair over his forehead and it was then that Maisie said again, 'Come in,' stepping back so the other two were forced to do the same.

Once in her tiny kitchen he immediately dominated it, the black leather jacket and black trousers he was wearing adding to the aura of brooding masculinity. Maisie swallowed. She still couldn't believe this was happening. Thank goodness she'd made an effort with her hair and put some make-up on this morning in honour of Sue and Jackie's arrival. She had thought if she looked reasonably good it wouldn't be so much of a 'poor Maisie' weekend. Her mouth was dry with shock and she swallowed again before she turned to her friends. 'I'll be all right,' she said weakly. 'Please, go through to the sitting room.'

'You don't look all right.' Sue was really into the British bulldog role.

'I am. Please, Jackie.' Maisie looked at Jackie and the other girl answered the appeal by taking Sue's arm and yanking her out of the kitchen.

'Sit…sit down.' Maisie gestured to one of the stools before hastily placing the girls' coffee and cheesecake on a tray. 'I'll just take this to them.'

Blaine didn't sit, neither did he say anything more. He just looked at her and something in his gaze made hot colour flood her face. She hurriedly left the kitchen, walking into the sitting room where Sue and Jackie were both standing poised like lionesses ready to protect their young. 'Sit down,' she whispered. 'Have your coffee. I'll call if I need you.'

'Promise?' Sue said grimly.

'Sue, he isn't about to attack me or anything,' Maisie said a bit more strongly. 'He's obviously come about something, so the least I can do is to hear what he has to say. Is Guiseppe all right?' she suddenly added to Jackie as the awful thought struck that maybe Blaine had come to tell her bad news.

Jackie nodded silently.

But it could be Humphrey or even the little foal. He might not have come to see *her*, not in that way. She turned quickly and, once in the kitchen again, saw that Blaine hadn't moved. She stood just inside the door, totally at a loss on how to handle what had become a surreal situation. And Blaine still didn't say anything. Her hands in fists with nerves, Maisie blurted, 'Is Humphrey all right?'

'Humphrey?' Blaine stared at her as though he didn't have a clue what she was on about.

'I...I thought you might have come to tell me Humphrey was ill. Or the foal.'

Blaine swore softly. 'Damn Humphrey. I have come to see *you*.'

The spark of hope that had flared deep inside when she had first seen him at the door re-ignited. 'Why?' she whispered.

'Do you have to ask?' He reached her in one stride, taking her in his arms and crushing her into him. 'Because I have finally come to my senses and I have been praying for days that it is not too late. Every minute we have been apart I have died a little. I cannot live without you, *mia piccola*. I do not *want* to live without you. Love hit me the minute you walked into that café with your hair tousled and your face pink and an uncertain smile on your face. I have been fighting it ever since.'

'You…don't love me.' She pulled back a little. She couldn't believe this. It would be too crushing, too devastating when she realised she'd got it wrong. She wouldn't be able to recover again. 'You said so. You don't want to be with one woman—'

'I don't want to be with any woman but you.' His mouth sought hers and he kissed her until her head swam. 'I have never felt like this in my life; you must believe that. And it happened like that.' He clicked his fingers. 'Instantly. And it scared me to death. I knew I could not let you go but I was scared to let you in too, so I devised the perfect plan. You would come to Italy and take care of things for my mother. I would be able to be with you and this ridiculous thing I was feeling would burn itself out. Only it did not happen like that. The more I was with you, the more I loved you, and the more I loved you the more frightened I became. It is not nice, eh, to discover the man you thought you loved is a coward?'

'You're not a coward,' she said shakily.

'*Sì*, Maisie, it is so. And it was not altogether my experience with Francesca that was holding me back. I must be honest if there is any hope for us. With Francesca, she did not touch here—' he placed her hand over his heart and she could feel he was trembling '—and I knew this as time went on. You were different. From the moment I met you I knew the power you had over me was too much, too dangerous. You would be able to break me. That is what I could not handle.'

She stared up at him, something starting to sing deep inside. 'But I would never do that,' she murmured. 'I would rather die than do that. I love you.'

He stroked his hand over her hair, along her cheek. 'But how could I trust that this would be so?' he said softly. 'We had only met three months ago, I told myself. This is madness. I had a good life, an acceptable life. My needs were met—' her eyelids flickered but still he went on '—I lived as I wanted to live and answered to no one. If I wanted to take off on a whim I could. No consultations, no compromise. I had my freedom and I lacked nothing. Why would I let all this go and only gain the potential to be hurt beyond measure in return? It was not logical or sensible. Why would I do that?'

'Why would you?' she whispered.

'Because it was all ashes without you.'

He was holding her small hands in his strong brown ones and as he drew her into him again a sob burst from her throat. 'But are you sure?' He had talked of getting hurt but he had already hurt her more than anyone else in the world. She could only take so much.

'I love you, Maisie. I want to marry you, have children, dogs, cats, anything you want. A house like the painting, *sì*? Where you will grow brown in the sun with our children and wait in the doorway for me to come home at the end of the day. This all happened too suddenly for me and I understand that now, but that's the way it is sometimes. I have known many other women, *mia piccola*, but none of them have ever stirred in me even a shadow of what I feel for you. I shall regret the heartache I have caused you to my dying day and I can never make up for the harm I have done, but I beg you, I beg you to trust me now. If you love me, believe me. Take me on faith. That is what love is all about, after all.'

Tears were raining down her face now. 'I'm afraid this is just a dream.'

'No, it is real. I am real.' His mouth took hers and he kissed her with gentle reassurance at first, then with rising ardour, his hands moving over her body with sensual purpose. 'Will you marry me, Maisie?' he said at last as he lifted his lips from hers. 'Will you be my wife?'

She looked into the beautiful greeny-blue eyes and this time there was no mask to hide how he felt. All the love in the world was there staring at her, beseeching her, wanting her, needing her.

She wrapped her arms round his neck and took the step of faith he had asked for. 'Yes,' she said, her eyes shining and her face aglow. 'Oh, yes, yes, yes.'

It was a Christmas wedding, all shades of cream and red and gold. Maisie looked more beautiful than any woman had ever looked since the beginning of time, according to Blaine, as she floated down the aisle of the little Italian church in a long full gown of cream silk with tiny gold pearls trimming the bodice and flowing veil. She carried a small posy of Christmas berries and tiny gold orchids, ribbons of cream and gold entwined through them. Sue and Jackie—or the blood-hounds, as Blaine had teasingly nicknamed her two best friends—marched proudly behind her in red silk, their Cheshire cat grins announcing how thrilled they were about everything.

Maisie's mother and most of her relations had been flown out to Italy by Blaine for the nuptials. Maisie had now risen to dizzy heights in their opinion after landing such a magnificent catch and so things were easier between Maisie and her mother. Just in case Susan Burns forgot, however, and slipped back into her old ways, Blaine's piercing gaze was there to remind his mother-in-law that his wife *would* be treated with the utmost respect.

Jenny had been ecstatic and distinctly weepy for weeks and even Guiseppe had damp eyes when the two took their vows, their voices ringing with love. It was a perfect wedding, everyone said, just perfect. And even the weather joined in the celebrations, the air mild and bright sunshine spilling out over the happy couple and their guests as they ate the wedding breakfast in the huge marquee in the garden of Jenny and Guiseppe's villa on Christmas Eve afternoon.

Blaine looked down at Humphrey who, as ever, was parked firmly at Maisie's feet, or on one satin-clad shoe to be exact. 'Have you noticed the tag on his collar?' he murmured in her ear.

She looked into her husband's beautiful eyes. 'How could I notice anything or anyone but you today?' she whispered back.

Blaine grinned. 'Right answer.' He bent down and lifted the little dog on to his lap, where Humphrey sat looking rather surprised at the unexpected bonus. He was a lot nearer the source of the wonderful smells which had been drifting down from the laden table here.

'Look.' Blaine lifted the large Christmas tag fixed to the collar Maisie had given Humphrey before she had left Italy at the end of the summer.

Maisie bent closer, receiving a quick lick from Humphrey who smelt wonderful having been bathed and coiffured for the occasion. He had submitted to all the ministrations with good grace, knowing he had got one over on all the other dogs—not to mention the cats—who had all been banned to the stables for the afternoon.

This is a special gift from me to you on your wedding day, darling. He loves you far more than me and is longing to be an only dog with no competition, if only for a little while before you fill your new house with more dogs and cats and babies. All my love, your other mum.

'She has given me Humphrey?' Maisie raised shining eyes to those of her husband.

Blaine nodded. 'But the arrangement is she is keeping him until we get back from honeymoon.' They were leaving for the Caribbean for a month's honeymoon the day after Boxing Day.

'Oh, Blaine.' Maisie wanted to cry with sheer happiness. Humphrey was such a special little dog and now he was hers.

'I know.' Blaine grinned at her. 'All this—me, roses round the door and now Humphrey too.'

She didn't mind that he was teasing her, not when he looked at her like he was looking at her now. She reached over Humphrey's furry head and kissed Blaine hard on the mouth. 'This is the best Christmas ever, Signor Morosini,' she murmured. 'And I love you more than words can say.'

'And you are the most beautiful bride ever, Signora Morosini, and I intend to show you how much I love you over and over again all night,' he said softly, his voice smoky with desire.

'Good.' There was no shyness in her brown eyes as she smiled at him, only a deep longing for the time when they would be alone in their big bed and she would finally be joined to him in body as well as heart and soul and mind. 'I've waited a long time for this, you know!'

'I do know.' Suddenly all the laughter was gone from his dark face. 'And I do not know what I have done to deserve you, my precious, sweet, honest, funny, beautiful Maisie. But I will spend the rest of my life making you happy. Do you believe this?'

'Of course I believe it.' And she did with all her heart. They had come through deep waters, they had weathered the storm and now love was at the helm.

It didn't get any better than that.

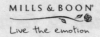

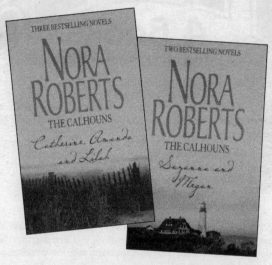

FREE!

4 Books
and a surprise gift!

We would like to take this opportunity to thank you for reading this Mills & Boon® book by offering you the chance to take FOUR more specially selected titles from the Modern Romance™ series absolutely FREE! We're also making this offer to introduce you to the benefits of the Mills & Boon® Reader Service™—

- ★ FREE home delivery
- ★ FREE gifts and competitions
- ★ FREE monthly Newsletter
- ★ Exclusive Reader Service offers
- ★ Books available before they're in the shops

Accepting these FREE books and gift places you under no obligation to buy, you may cancel at any time, even after receiving your free shipment. Simply complete your details below and return the entire page to the address below. You don't even need a stamp!

YES! Please send me 4 free Modern Romance books and a surprise gift. I understand that unless you hear from me, I will receive 6 superb new titles every month for just £2.80 each, postage and packing free. I am under no obligation to purchase any books and may cancel my subscription at any time. The free books and gift will be mine to keep in any case.

P6ZEF

Ms/Mrs/Miss/Mr ....Initials..
                                                        BLOCK CAPITALS PLEASE
Surname ....
Address ....

....
....Postcode ....

Send this whole page to:
UK: FREEPOST CN81, Croydon, CR9 3WZ